# After Pie

## by Stefan Petrucha

Though Barbie's arms are made so they cannot move, to keep our girl-children humble, she and Ken are happy to be pressed together in an expression of their stiff love. That is, until the unexpected arrival of a tag sale GI Joe with better muscle definition and a superior selection of movable joints.

There is no overt seduction, no conscious attempt on Joe's part to thwart Ken and Barbie's monogamy as thanks for his service. Nonetheless, inevitably, his real-life hair and darling cheek-scar turn a certain someone's poseable head. And one hot, steamy moment, while Ken is off Malibu surfing, hoping to find his purpose among the imaginary waves, back in the welcoming dollhouse, the plastic surface tension gets to be too much.

Brutish Joe approaches Barbie, and though able to speak 16 phrases through the holes in his chest, he is wordless. In silence, his painted eyes lock on her tight career girl outfit in a way that makes her ache. All it takes is a touch of his Kung-Fu grip, with fingers you open and let close, on her slender, ultra-white 22 shoulder, and she begs to turn herself over to him.

Alas, it's all for naught.

Having no genitalia, all they can do is go mad with longing. In this, a returning Ken joins in, aspiring to be a ménage à trois. Nonetheless, they remain impotent. Enraged by their hobbled lust, the three turn to darker faiths, worshipping one elder god after another, seeking any supernal power that, no matter how vile, can make them real. Yet no matter how they debase and prostrate themselves before rotation-molded images, no matter what toys they sacrifice, from plastic dogs to plastic babies, they never find salvation. Never. And since plastic, though organic, does not decompose, never is much longer for them than it is for you or I.

The end.

# Why After Pie?

Because…
The meal is done.
Dessert is over.
And the long night begins.

# 1

We hunt the ghosts.
We hunt ourselves.

The dark does not deter us, nor the constant threat of the invisible, for we know what the light-dwellers never will; that only in hunting the unseen, in being unseen ourselves, do we truly live. Not in high school halls, or failing malls, or online ass-lying living room squalls, finger-ticking our meaninglessness into some spider's cosmic World Wide Web, but here, in the phoneless, grid-less dark. It is here, on these dust-creaky floorboards, that we live in the ancient, bone-deep sense, the true sense, the sense of not merely being, but of being aware that we are.

Or... it could just be a fad.

Not having ghost-hunted before, I can't say how long my paranormal phase will last. Heart of hearts? I could be back on a comfy bedroom floor tomorrow, playing with Barbies named Flotsam and Jetsam, while Beep lies on her unmade bed tapping her star-painted toes to music only she can hear.

Because she's wearing earbuds, not because she's schizo or anything.

Yet, having come thus far, dare I return so soon to that shallow ignorance?

Sure, what the hell. Why not? There's nothing wrong with taking a step back, as long as it's part of the dance. Yeah, they say you can't go home again, but I call stinky-time bullshit. Home may be the only thing you can go back to, especially in this job market and Beep's such a short walk—just a few blocks. I could head on back there any time.

I figure I'm supposed to tell you my name, but Beep does it for me when she says, "Shelley, you hear that?"

I tsk like tsking's going out of style, which, by the way, it has. Her question is too vague to elicit a useful response. In this cracker-box McMansion, with its whispers, whooshes, rustles and ticks, *that* could mean a million things. Regardless of intent, her question only serves to frustrate. It would be rude of me *not* to be irritated.

When my tsk fails to illuminate the problem, I turn back toward Beep and her placid ignorance. Despite best efforts to render my gaze doll-dead, it retains a spark, with which I give a long, slow eye-roll.

She got her nick-*nom* (as in *de plume*) because I once put my finger to her nose, said, "Beep" and it stuck. No, we weren't little kids. It was yesterday, which means I've been calling her Beep for nearly a day. An infinity of time, if you're looking at a drop of water.

If you're not, maybe you should.

The moniker will change, no doubt. I'll forget it, or it'll evolve, as if on its own, to Boop, or Bloop or Blorp, or a homier, Bee. Here in the town of Blear, whatever can stick doesn't do so for long. It's like the song—we sacrifice our lions to the lambs.

Or something. I hate repeating lyrics.

Da-da-da, a whiter shade of white on white?

Long short, tomorrow, I may call her Jelly. Next week, I may not call her at all. Especially if she doesn't get her ass in gear and tell me what the fuck she meant by *that*.

In a final effort to grease the cerebral wheels, I say unto her, "Beep, what the fuck do you mean by *that*?"

Her sweeping digit covers an infinite number of dusty, midair points. She says again, with more emphasis:

"That!"

I glare, wordless, until at last, realization dawns and Beep gets with the program. Her pointing narrows, indicating the general direction of the upscale kitchen. Her words get more specific, too:

"That low moan, like a refrigerator, only there's no electricity."

I hear it now. Maybe I always did but lacked a need to focus. Once I'm not missing it, it's hard to miss. Loud and low, it invades my lower molars, nestling in a spot my tongue can't reach, like a vibrating piece of bacon.

I'd like to say that shit gets real, but it is just a hum, a weird, moany hum, yes, but a hum. Still, I have to push Beep to get myself moving through this shadow-swallowed entry hall, toward the sound of origins as-yet unknown.

You know, to hunt the ghosts.

As we creep into the creepy, I mourn that fact that after so many years together, we share no BFF bond to carry my thoughts across the thin air and into her thick, and often numb, skull. I shouldn't have had to glare at all. My tsk should have spoken volumes. A freaking stranger would've known what it meant.

Thing is, of late I wish a stranger *were* here, and not her.

When growing up in a coziness which you're expected to accept with gratitude, (because other children starve and the world is full of weeping which we don't understand), friendship is a question of proximity over choice.

At least until you can drive.

Having acquired my learner's permit, I've taken to wonder, not only whether Beep is but a companion of convenience, but also, with such comfort food perpetually reminding me how clever I am, how much of myself, or the ghosts, I can truly hope to hunt.

Sadly, though, she'd be my hanger-on no matter where we lived, and with good reason. We both know full well that I am a natural born leader, and, not only whip-smart, but, to the discerning, quite the bit of eye-rolling, eye-candy.

On the lighter side, Beep's not so bad herself, if you know what I mean, and she is, above all else, here, the one I shove to get myself moving. So, that's something I guess.

We'll see. Road test in three weeks.

Baby LEDs in hand, we pass beyond the entry hall. The drywall palace has been empty a while, but not nearly long enough for nature to reclaim. Among the departed's privileged accoutrement remain the sad echoes of recessed lighting, the bones of electric angels high up in the cathedral ceilings. The

"To be honest, I wanted to. I probably would have, but..."

Silence needn't be awkward, but this one is.

"What? As Blake tells us, Beep, sooner murder an infant in its cradle than nurse unacted desires. There weren't any infants around, so why not carpe ickum?"

An odd laugh-cry shivers her timbers. "Because *you* suggested it."

My hand pats the "o" of my mouth. "Do you think I'd ever do anything to hurt you?"

"Yes. Why should today be different? Besides, we needed a designated driver."

Taking in this vile, yet accurate, insult, I nod a bit too much. And to think I was willing to fake a certain fondness toward her. Ignorance of Beep is bliss. Besides, I have a new friend now.

I lean into the open back window, sensually lowering myself until I'm up to the elbows in ick, no doubt looking like an oil-soaked playmate of the month.

The teen teetotaler watches. "What do you think you're doing?"

Don't know why I bother, but I lie, shielding her from an emotional/physical/spiritual affair that would no doubt hurt her gravely.

"Oh, just trying to give ick a better view."

"I can't believe you touch it. How do you even know where its eyes are?"

Then, I figure, no, I want to rub her face in it.

"Because, my naïve pseudo-ingenue, while you've been off in little Bo-Beep-land, thinking your little Bo-Beep-thoughts, in your little Bo-Beep-way, ick and I have been developing an interspecies rapport, right here, behind your smooth and shapely back!"

"Tch. You have not."

My hot body drips goo, my husky voice, poison. "Do try not to be jealous. Ick and I could do without petty distraction."

Her face reminds me of Charlie Brown's when it has that little squiggle for lips. "Jealous? I'd love it if you *did* talk to... ick. I'm just afraid you're making up more and more stuff up as floor plan is open, party-friendly, the kitchen both one with and separate from the so-called "living" room, not unlike a holy Trinity minus one.

With one less wall between us and the hum, it's louder, hummier, if you will, its wavering pitch more clearly changing, rising and falling, like a sigh on a sigh. But in the kitchen, things are much worse than Beep or I imagined, or much better, depending on your goal.

Not only is the electricity off, there's no refrigerator.

Oh, there was, once, a big one, large enough to hold any number of troped refrigerator girls, killed to enhance the meaning of her man. I'm talking two doors and a deep freezer drawer at least, but all that remains of it, stove or dishwasher, are the pre-sized hollows whose darkness seems to weep for their toppled Amana kings and queens.

Judging by the torn CAT cable tied along a copper water feed, and the matching jacks on the 220v wall plates, the absent appliances were Internet-enabled, smart machines. Not smart enough, though, were you? Look upon my recipes, ye mighty, and this chair.

Because, there's this chair. And I'm looking at it because it's the *only* piece of furniture in the place. It sits on its lonesome in the whining and dining nook, as if awaiting a tired hapless fool to rest therein, that it might transport them to some dark-stained dimension for its giant chair-masters to feed upon.

But Beep's shaking, my molars aching and the question remains; do smart refrigerators dream of electric hums? Is it the ghost of a machine we hear?

If not, what *is* making that noise?

Word is the bank foreclosed when the owners lost their none-of-my business. Still, I've heard that within these walls an entirely different sort of business remains unfinished, that here Satan worshippers culled the local daycare herd, engaging in ritual emotional abuse; that here, unrequited love led to incest, madness and sudden death; that here, crippling childhood diseases were treated not by pill, but by pillow, heavily pressed for as long as symptoms persist. Cruelty, in short, beyond what any would consider human.

Because there *must* be limits to human cruelty, no?

How the weird hum ties in, I've no idea. The best ghost-hunters know it's foolish to make assumptions without evidence. Don't they? Perhaps I'm thinking only of myself.

As we approach the hollow, it gets louder. Ever the scientist, I test it, taking a few steps back, shoving Beep a few steps closer. Indeed, it grows softer with the distance.

"At least it's not following us," I tell Beep.

She nods. I doubt she has any idea what she's agreeing with, but if it comforts her, I see no reason to rob her of that. Humanity cannot bear too much reality. Beep, less than most.

When I toe forward once more, the hum grows so clear it ruins everything.

Damn. It's not coming from the fridge-grave, it's coming from a window to the left, where what's left of the rain bitch-slaps the pane. In other words, it's not coming from the beyond, but from outside.

I see what's making the noise now, but lay it out, motioning for Beep to open the sliding doors. We step onto the deck and into a wet wind. I'll give it this, in the free air it still sounds ghostly. Having already guessed the truth, though, the best imitation of pain-so-profound-it-outlives-biology wouldn't cheer me.

Wittily satirizing Beep's earlier *that*, I point up and say, "There."

She'd doesn't get the joke, but it's not her fault. Given where I point, there's not much to choose from. A coax cable runs along the wall, past the second floor, all the way to the tippy top. There, it shimmies out of sight behind a chim-chimney before stretching across the air to a street-pole, where it once connected the residents and their too-smart-for-their-own-good machines to the greater ignorance of the world.

Shorn of several clips, the cable has far more slack than it deserves. All flaccid and floppy, the wind whips it against the siding, producing the hum. Were nature inherently just, I'd think the cable was being punished. Were nature inherently into S&M, I'd think both were having a grand time.

True, a moan is not a noise you'd think a cable could make,

but there it is. There's some tangential cosine plus or minus thing involved, but that's as far as I go. I neither know nor care about this part of science.

To be sure, I have Beep test it by grabbing the coax and snapping her wrist. It sounds as if she's goosed a humming ghost. We chuckle briefly. mystery solved, but the big questions, as always, are left unanswered.

Still tilted roof-ward, I note a few stars poking from the dissipating clouds. Damn stars, couldn't care less, and if they did, they wouldn't get me any more than Beep does. At least I never thought they did, until this happens:

Light.

A big one, way up there, and moving fast. Not just moving. Like the opening of Pynchon's *Gravity's Rainbow*, it screams across the sky. He was talking about a Nazi rocket. Me, I have no idea what I'm talking about.

I mean, what the hell is that?

"Holy shit," Beep says, a phrase I've never quite understood.

Still, I find myself agreeing. If anything covers the expanse between the hallowed and the profane it's this. Holy shit.

Its shape? A light. It's color? White, but I'm not one of those who can see Mars as red from down here. It's tinged, with maybe... I want to say blue, but then it looks more yellow.

I could ask Beep, but don't want someone else's words, especially hers, interfering with this. My senses magnified by an adrenaline-filled, car accident slo-mo, I can't be sure how long it screams, but not so long that I have to blink. Large among the smattering of eager speck-stars, it offers no further sense of scale, until it yowls behind the tree line hugging the cul de sac.

And—boomf.

Not boom. Boomf.

While it has many characteristics of a classic deep, hollow, boom, there is, at the very end, the audible whisper of an afterthought, like a giant powderpuff hitting a gargantuan tin of makeup, or the final swing in a sexy pillow-fight of the gods.

There's definitely an *f* at the end. Boomf.

I'd like to report that flames or sparks follow, but everything just stops—lights-out, all gone, save for the little red artifacts produced by my still-startled retinas.

Gone as it is, I stare at where it was.

"Beep," I say, "Maybe we shouldn't be hunting ghosts. Maybe we should be hunting aliens."

# 2

We hunt the aliens.
　　　We hunt ourselves.

Fear of the other does not deter us, we seek to become it. For we know it is not in this hollow world that we can touch our true-selves' sky, but out there, that-away, in the implacable distance, among the starry-stars.

Gort, Klaatu borada nikto.

No doubt some will ask if a cisgenre switch renders my narration unreliable. Not at all. You can count on me. I am tried and true. But understand, it's not my fault things change.

My permission is unrequited.

In either case, it remains the stuff of night that beckons. In science fiction, the panoply of pin-prick lights, in horror, the dark between them. The difference? Location, location, location.

Abandoned by the screaming, the wind-whipped coax continues its fake spirit plea.

"Let's go see," Beep says.

She doesn't mean it. She's too small for such thoughts. I must push her to push myself. That's our rule, our glue that binds. Or not. In a heinous breach of our interpersonal hegemony, her hands abandon the deck and she Beep-lines across the tawny lawn. With her AWOL, the only pushing I do is to keep up.

Oh, Beep, we'll have to sit down later, you and I, and have ourselves a good heart-to-heart about these disturbing displays of proactivity.

Rest assured, despite her giddy-girl speed, I reach the asphalt first.

In some other direction, the road may go ever on. Here,

the Lincoln Way cul-de-sac terminates both physically and culturally. McCracker mansions man-splay the perimeter like manicured couch potatoes. The faux haunter we left behind was the only spud among them ever completed, leaving these posers half-baked beneath streetlight husks that shed dead wiring instead of illumination. Not that there's *no* light. Of a sudden, there's plenty, more than enough to leave us squinting. A gaudy rush of artificial reds is coming fast, backed by the screech of skidding tires in tones more wet than rubbery. They puddle-swish straight at us.

"Geezit, the cops!" I say.

We high-tail it, hoping to blow this burg without getting pinched, but my delight at my noir anachronisms is brief, exchanged for an equally delightful fear. You see, I'm thinking this is all about me, punishment for trespassing against others as I'd have others trespass against me. I'm thinking I must be top of their most wanted list, not simply wanted, but *needed*, a way for hard-working blue-boys to make their careers, a way to give them that tale they can one day tell their mutant grandkids as they sit pie-wide-eyed on their surprisingly supple replacement knees.

Nope. My importance, is, as usual, imagined. Like the stars, the me-first responders (I can't tell if it's the police) care not for me. They blur past, oblivious to the glass-shard evidence of our breaking and entering, not even slowing to check out the eye candy.

It's an insult, I tell you. They're after the light. Meaning... they seek the aliens.

Ah... but do they seek themselves?

They tear through the yard right across from us, equally heedless of the landscaping, itself a crime worth prosecution. Narrowly missing the house itself, they swerve around back, single-file, racing beyond the property line to vanish among the wooded hills.

Wooded hills, which now I note, are smoking like a pack a day.

With such manly tire tracks providing virile breadcrumbs, what woman could refuse?

Lest Beep again steal my leading-lady line, I tell her, "Come on."

The treasure-map lines gouged in the lawn take us to a dirt road. Not just dirt, it's filthy. If not for a fallen chain and rotted "DO NOT" sign, I'd think the drivers only imagined a path here, that they're still making one up as they go along.

Dauntless, we proceed, entering a forbidden land of hirsute tree-trunks and pulpy ground.

Blear calls itself the *land of a thousand picnic tables*, but this is no walk in the park. Moist earth slurps twixt shoe and dainty sock, needlessly pointy rocks stab my eternal rubber soles. Worse, while the not-haunted house innards succumbed to our LEDs, this more natural dark renders them useless, unable to pierce a thing, leaving so very much impossible to see.

A man might feel emasculated by this. We do not have that luxury.

In short order, direction becomes subjective, but, when isn't it, really? Yes, I still hear gunning engines, and, yes, to Americans such as us, that has a certain erotic charge, but the hubbub does nothing to guide us. Humans suck at localizing low-frequency sound. It's why growling tigers can sneak up on us, why home audio only requires a single bass speaker.

We are built to be fooled.

It almost makes me sympathetic to Beep's earlier sound descriptor of *that*. Almost.

Fortunately, light is another matter, or rather, another form of matter. The thickening smoke, strobed and stroked by emergency lights may reduce reality to a gaudy Hollywood cliché, but it does provide direction: up and over some great big hills of hope, or whatever that means.

"Once more into the Sneetch," I say. "Get it, Beep?"

"Shakespeare and Seuss," she replies.

"Stop thinking you're smart," I warn. "It only leads to trouble."

The steeper angle makes for a harder slog, but where I come from, Sisyphus is another word for sissy. My companion nose-breathes heavily, probably to conceal how hard her sweet bod is working at the climb, but, bless and/or damn her soul, she does not slow a whit.

Making it incumbent on me to move faster and pretend a greater endurance.

At last we encounter evidence that the boomf-site nears; a glowing trail of trees, hacked lower and lower as if by celestial scythe. Here, nature itself grows impure. Not from radiation or time-space rifts, from trash. Not the kind you talk, the kind that simply is. Beer cans and liquor bottles, indigenous to the area, are among the expected denizens. The half-buried shopping cart juting from a pile of dead leaves like the head of Ozymandias risen from the sands of time, is rarer, but hardly aberrant. The baby carriage, glinting wherever the rust isn't too thick, is more a puzzler.

Was it thrown out with or without the baby? And what of the bathwater?

In the hope it is not just some stupid meteorite up ahead, that unlike this junk, something more than heaven's detritus masquerading as purpose lies ahead, I vow not to be distracted.

Right before I'm about to find out, my foot hits something squishy and round that sends me falling on my face: a red rubber ball. How dare it, with me so close to claiming my hard-won goosey gander? Yet, all that's left is to raise my head from the muck.

For some reason, I can't.

Instead, my vow to stay focused slips off between the crenellations of my insect mind and I keep looking at the ball, this Eden-apple that made me fall, this tripster beside my foot. My brain disgorges some nonsense about a connection between the throwaway ball and my throw-away self. Puerile even for me, it ricochets hard against the moment.

And all the while, Beep, damn Beep, cursed Beep, a pox upon her and her heirs, is on her feet and staring into the precious light. I can tell from her face it's no moaning cable, it's something so real it's unreal. Her face lit with rapture is all the petty motive I need. I force my buzzcut mind aside and snap my head up, eager to see what's beyond this pale predictable happenstance that calls itself a world. Only I can't take it.

Seeing, I mean.

Before I can crack the doors of perception, to harvest my

field of vision, I go back, cowardly and ashamed, knocked on my smart-ass, reduced to glaring at the earthy-ball below.

It's as if a cosmic Slurpee has given me brain-freeze.

Why? What's with me? What's left me? I can't be that broken, I can't be, unless…

*Is there method to my madness?* the mad girl asks.

Of course. That must be it. If I think I have purpose, I must— Cogito finem habere, ergo facio. If it's me, it must be a great purpose indeed. And, as we all know, great purpose brings great irresponsibility. But what might it be?

Well… maybe I'm not scared shitless. Maybe instead, I feel a selfless noblesse oblige to prepare you, my gentle readers, for what's atop that hill, to ground the ground so you can kiss the sky, to bring you into this moment for realsies.

How best to do that? Simple, by taking this nothing ball and suddenly making it all seem worthwhile, to bouncy-bounce it from passing irrelevance to something sublime, allowing you to better grasp what comes next. After all, if language can't conjure such a simple thing, what's the point of trying to get across the good stuff?

That's my story, and I'm sticking to it. I am donning my glass slipper to take you to the ball, to tiptoe it from word-map to world-terrain.

Nothing up my sleeve, I begin with what I see on bended mud-soaked knee; branching cracks on a peeling surface, an inner porous pink exposed like viscera beneath skin, two deeper holes where something like a dog chewed upon it mightily. It smells of rotted leaves mixed with a childhood memory. What of the other senses? Should I touch it, or pop it in my mouth, to tell you how it tastes against my tongue or squished twixt my teeth?

Dare I eat a ball?

But if I do, what will you do with it? You are the other half of this letter to the world, y'know. Why is it all on me? Why can't I just say, screw it, it's a damn red, rubber ball? Why not let you be the ball?

And if you won't, why should I?

Please, please, see the ball, one way or the other. Know that it's real, that this place and moment are real. Know that sad, small thing, and I swear the rest will fall into place. It has to, because, like it or not, ball and boomf, mud and stars, share the same reality, and, ipso facto, ergo, can't be *completely* different, can they?

Ready? Set? Go. This time, for sure.

I stand, eyes locked, but not weak-kneed. What once Slurpee-froze now leaves my brain aflame. After spewing all that crap about the ball, I die with self-loathing for using a word like *thing*, yet I'm consumed with the question: What the fuck *is* this thing?

Words flail, but don't quite surrender. Kamikaze nouns, shielded by frail adjectives, hurl themselves against reality's edge, exploding in an act of faith, a clinging to a baseless belief that if enough false-analogies sacrifice themselves, their battered corpses might yield at least a vague outline of the prize.

So, what the fuck *is* this thing?

It is… ick, mostly. If the 9 billion living miracles of the human body are 75% water, this puppy's 90% snot. But snot if snot were not so banal. How ick is it? It's so ick, it's like the wet dream of the one true god, the ejaculate the Egyptian deity Atum used to create the cosmos.

Look it up, it's a guy thing. How else can a man give birth?

I'll try again. You know the turtles that carry the universe on their backs? Turtles all the way down? It's as if they had a bad head cold, but drank enough water to render their mucous translucent, free of the greens or yellows that indicate infection or at least a high pollen count.

Ask your doctor. I will not speak with mine. Not after this.

Ick, ubiquitous ick, ultimate ick, dangling and oozing, pulsing and popping, dripping and drooping, sliming and shining, dirtying the dirt, licking the tree trucks, seeping so deep into my mind that my earliest childhood memories now have goo on them.

And, good golly, Miss Molly, mommy is not going to clean this shit up.

The remaining 10%, the solid bits, the dried snot in the flotsam, are bony, maybe, fishlike, if they are, the sort you pull from your teeth when eating seafood, only not that stiff or organized. These are more like the overachieving white hairs on an old man's crazy eyebrows, too frail to provide shape.

It's not at all like the ball. I've seen balls before. Not this, though. Though armed only with ass-making assumption, we must go on, I'll go on.

Is it what we might consider alive? How the hell should I know? There is a whole lot of twitchy going on. If movements that seem *deliberate* are an indication, yea, though I walk through the uncanny valley, sure, let's call it alive. If nothing else, it lets me call the rest, not-alive. That could mean inorganic, dormant, or Polly gone to meet his maker dead, but at least alive/not alive lets us, hand in hand, giddily leap to another assumption, based entirely on cliché science fiction tropes:

Having screamed across the stars to boomf here, the un-living parts are likely the container, the old timey Cracker-Jacks box, if you will. The living ooze is the prize hidden inside.

What we have here, is a spacecraft and its alien occupant.

True? Who knows. It could be a divine candy wrapper, the litter of the gods, but you have to start somewhere. There is some additional evidence backing up the spaceship theory, or at least, in the hands of a clever attorney, it can be made to do so.

For instance, the not-alive part is cracked. No, not like the ball. Forget the ball already, will you? It's cracked open, but more like a geode than an eggshell. Smoking and tree-scuffed, it cups, protects and holds, the brighter area within which licks much of the aforementioned ick-movement. The movement of...?

Limbs? Sure. What the hell, why not? Arms, legs, maybe, pseudopodia, maybe something new, borrowed or blue.

You'd think my fellow humans, the we-happy-crew of first responders, aka the authorities, would be easier to explain, but they're not. They're easier to *recognize*, sure, but that only makes them harder to explain.

Freaking me out nearly as much as the goo, they're yanking away at the maybe-limbs as if it's their good buddy Joe stuck in that-thar geode and they gotta get him before the whole thing blows—despite the fact they've no idea if any of this is safe to touch, or so much as which quivering end of the ick is up.

In a rare occurrence, Beep gets it, too. Barely audible above the fart noises resulting from their ick-mucking, she whispers, "Should they be doing that?"

"No, Beep, they should not. What we have here is a failure to assimilate."

As mentioned, thinking it's a spacecraft is already a leap. How do they know those bony limb-things are the point? What if the pilot *is* the goo? What if they're scraping off an intelligent being, and giving all their loving care and attention to a houseplant it brought along to spruce the place up a little?

For pity's sake, doesn't this strange visitor from another planet have certain alien rights?

Sometimes I have to wonder which does more damage; evil or incompetence? Sure, evil gives you spiritual cooties, but if you're talking pure numbers, I suspect it's a close fucking race.

Maybe these idgit galoots are amateurs, weekend volunteer Hazmat personnel. Maybe they were waist-deep in a local dive bar, monitoring police bands and drunk-drove out here on a bet. In a rare occurrence, my concerns are echoed by a disembodied voice.

Squawking from a car radio, it begs, "Keep back!"

It goes on to threaten job loss, prison, and impossible rape-like acts, forcing me to conclude they *do* work for someone.

Drunk as skunks, lost in the moment's mud, they pay no never mind.

Beep, her eyes flying-saucer wide, says, "The falcon cannot hear the falconer."

And I'm all like, "Whoa! You pick *now* to say something insightful? You mean all this time, we could have been having actual conversations?"

Her quick fall to silence confirms that I am essentially alone.

To top it all off, one of the rescue crew starts peeling off his pants. Then another.

Okay. We're beyond stupid now, into some new terrain.

They don't just look buzzed, they look.... *ecstatic*, like the goo is the best dessert-pie ever, or more, that it's something so very, very good you have to save it for later.

After pie, to coin a phrase.

Maybe they're *not* idiots, or not *just* idiots. Maybe touching that ick is so damn *amazing*, they want to feel it all over regardless of consequence, particularly the groin area, given they've kept their shirts on.

Which, y'know, makes *me* want to climb on in and cop a feel.

Hey, I never metanoia I didn't like.

"Should we...?" Beep asks.

"Hush," I say.

I admit to knowing little (which, technically, means knowing more than most, and certainly more than Beep) but one thing I do know is that the here and now, particularly *this* here and now, will soon be lost and gone forever, leaving it up to me to do what sanity would, if only it were here; to act, and act now, to stop them, or at least try.

That way, when the world's a burnt shell, its inhabitants destroyed by this goop that only wanted directions, I can say to the corpses: "See? I told you so."

Plus, I really, *really* want to touch that goo.

Telling myself it's time to put my money in my mouth, I jump, arms wide, to better wrap my destiny in a big ol' hug. I fly, as if in a dream where I can leap impossible distances. But I'm not dreaming. Rather than destiny, it's my density I embrace, face-planting the mud. Not giving up, I gracelessly spider-scramble the rest of the way.

Then, to what I imagine must be Beep's shock and chagrin, I'm out there, ready to touch all the things I should not, ready to rescue this wondrous extra-specialness from those who would keep it all for themselves, and, instead, keep it all for myself.

Reaching for what could be a hand, but for all I know are genitals, I say, "Come on, ick, we're moving."

Everyone stops dead, like, who the hell is this?

Which is pretty impressive, since I'm standing next to an EBE. Perhaps I am quite the eye candy after all. Only, no.

Wrong again. They're not looking *at* me, they're looking past me, straight at... Beep?

They're looking at... Beep? Why? Her ensemble doesn't go at

all with the mud. Haven't they seen a deer caught in headlights before? That goo must be some great shit.

Insulted as I am, I remain level-headed enough to realize that Beep has, for whatever inexplicable reason, provided a distraction, within which lies the precious time ick and I need to make our great escape.

I'd like to say that's what happened, that the ick and I ran off and had some amazing adventures you wouldn't believe, that we faced challenges that sorely tested, but did not defeat us, and, in the process of seeking our mutual survival, we bonded, advancing human-alien relations by eons (not the way you're thinking, gutter-mind), that it all ended in a tear-soaked departure that left us both, and the world, forever changed, but for the better.

Only I get this crazy clear, who-the-hell-are-you? 'tude— and it's coming from the ick.

Yeah, given its unknowable nature, I could be 16mm projecting, but I find myself overwhelmed with this terribly *specific* sense that ick's dying to speed-learn English, idioms, Oxford comma and all, just to express its deep offense at my interruption.

Boy, is my face red.

Not only that, now that my hand's right where it wanted to be, in the gloop, I don't see what the fuss is all about. It doesn't feel *especially* ick, or, like, much of anything. So why then is the goo-squad still so tickled and pants-less?

No fair, no fair!

Adding insult to injury, the ick yanks its whatever away.

Geez, it's not like I tried to put it in my mouth or anything.

"Oh, Beep, the prom is ruined, my sweet sixteen a shambles!" I tell her.

And she's like all, "What? How could you touch that…?"

And I'm like, "Where are your Yeats quotes now?"

Then the oh-so-sexy roar of more trucks butt-fucks the air. It hits the tush of night so hard it has to pull down its fly just to sneeze. I bet these guys are sober.

Fine. Whatever. Ick's loss, not mine. Must be lots of aliens out there, what with all those dots up in the sky.

"Let's amscray, toots," I say to Beep.

This time, the anachronism does not delight at all. It is ashes in my mouth.

With a nod as good as a wink, we run and run and run.

I don't even stop to pick up the ball.

# 3

Shelley, as Beep says whenever trying to get my deficit attention. My name is Shelley. I wish I could say I was named
after Mary Shelley, but I'm not.

Never mind. Scratch that. I don't wish I could say that at all.

*Frankenstein* sucked. Sure, Mary was a quite contrary literary
figure, and as a fellow woman (hey fellow, we're women!)
I should feel some allegiance, but I barely dragged myself
through that yawner. *Modern Prometheus* my ass. Where's the
fire? Once the monster could speak, he couldn't shut-up for the
artificial life of him.

*You made me so you owe me,* yap-yap-yap, credo of the modern
teen.

Beep, at least, can be silenced when spoken to. Besides, if you
want to name someone after Mary, try Wollstonecraft, surname
her feminist mom kept despite her marriage. Now, that, I could
get into. Perhaps I'll have Beep call me Wollstonecraft. She is
still Beep, apparently. The name has stuck for another day.

But I digest. Following last night's debacle, I wound up in
the dread-bed of Beep's little girl room, for the latest in what
seems a hellish eternity of slumber parties. Having toss-turned
aplenty, at some point I stop bemoaning my alien heartbreak
and tumble to sleep.

Rather than some intriguing psychedelia brought about by
a delayed reaction to the goo, I dream, of all things, about the
phone ringing. Heedless of my narrative the sound continues,
until at last, it hurts more than being awake. So, my eyes go
blink-blink, my toes go bouncy-bounce, and right in my middle,
as usual, it goes, "Aghhhhhh!"

I wakey-wake to wonder... was it just a dream?

Yep. Smartphone is battery-brain-dead. But there is a real sound, equally irritating, that perhaps my dream reimagined; a *tug-crack-tug-crack-tug* at the window. Has Poe's raven come to deny me balm in Gilead? (Like I'd ever look for balm in that two-bit town. I get mine online, sunshine.)

Oh-so curious, away to said window I fly like a flash, pretend to tear open the shutter (since there is none) and nearly throw-up on the sash. No jelly-belly, no good-girl gifts from a jolly-old pervert elf, just Beep, stuck on her own roof by a jammed frame.

At least now I know what time it is. Behind her, early morning brings the dew thing. Specks of water sparkle every which where, as if nature just emerged from the shower and has yet to grab a towel.

My waking brain's dewing the same (Get it? We have such fun with words, don't we?) shiny in specks, mostly dull and moist.

Beep continues to pry the window.

"Go away," I say to her.

"It's my room!" she says, as if she has a point.

"Then you shouldn't have gotten yourself stuck out there."

Alas, she succeeds.

I stick to my guns. "Get out, now."

"Forever is composed of nows," she says, paused on the outer sill.

I hiss like a punctured balloon. "Don't sweet-talk me. Just because you can quote Dickinson or Yeats or whatever doesn't mean you understand them, Beep."

Her pursed lips show gumption. "My name is...."

I raise my hand, ready to clamp her mouth. "No! This is my story. The only name you get is the one I give you."

Palm at the ready, I stare until she gives.

Think me a bully? Too bad. Think a main character should be all please love me, admire my descriptions, my world-building, my shapely arc, like I'm the new kid and you're some cool clique to be wooed?

Screw that noise.

Post alien rebuff, I don't care about much of anything. I

just want to write what I want to write the way I want to write it. Can't follow? Build some damn neurons, look stuff up on Wiki. Or better yet, stop reading my damn story. Because if I say something meaningful and you don't get it? That's on you. Reading is not a spectator sport.

Having thus restored the natural order, I nod for Beep to speak.

"Look, I know you don't usually talk to anyone except me, so I get how you're bummed because you think that... whatever, like, rebuffed you, but, seriously, you don't really know it was saying *anything*. You don't know *what* happened."

"I do."

An exhale. "Suppose you're right. It's not as if you're the only one who's ever been rejected."

"Yes, Beep. Yes, I am. The only one."

"Fine." She extends the *f* so long, it can only mean *fuck you*.

A gracious princess, I wave her further into her room. "Very well. Enter to play Barbies, freely and of your own will."

She does. We do. As the sun also rises, it's old times, a final youthful bender to help me forget, before my driving test brings childhood's end.

Though Barbie's arms are made so they *cannot* move, to keep our girl-children humble, she and Ken are happy to be pressed together in an expression of their stiff love. That is, until the unexpected arrival of a tag sale GI Joe with better muscle definition and a superior selection of movable joints.

There is no overt seduction, no conscious attempt on Joe's part to thwart Ken and Barbie's monogamy as thanks for his service. Nonetheless, inevitably, his real-life hair and darling cheek-scar turn a certain someone's poseable head. And one hot, steamy moment, while Ken is off Malibu surfing, hoping to find his purpose among the imaginary waves, back in the welcoming dollhouse, the plastic surface tension gets to be too much.

Brutish Joe approaches Barbie, and though able to speak 16 phrases through the holes in his chest, he is wordless. In silence, his painted eyes lock on her tight career girl outfit in a way that makes her ache. All it takes is a touch of his Kung-Fu grip, with fingers *you* open and let close, on her slender, ultra-white shoulder, and she begs to turn herself over to him.

Alas, it's all for naught.

Having no genitalia, all they can do is go mad with longing. In this, a returning Ken joins in, aspiring to be a *ménage à trois*. Nonetheless, they remain impotent. Enraged by their hobbled lust, the three turn to darker faiths, worshipping one elder god after another, seeking any supernal power that, no matter how vile, can make them real. Yet no matter how they debase and prostrate themselves before rotation-molded images, no matter what toys they sacrifice, from plastic dogs to plastic babies, they never find salvation. Never. And since plastic, though organic, does not decompose, never is much longer for them than it is for you or I.

The end.

Game over, we lie on the big girl bed in the little girl room, a mixed mess of toys and smells. I admit, I like that Beep is here. I like that she has a body. I like the thought of rubbing her neck or nudging her bare back with my bare shoulder.

Whatever dense, insipid assumptions you might have about my urges, I am not gay for Beep. Sex is not sensuality. Some get hard-ons from the wind, wet on horseback. Others do not. Deal with it. More important, most important, you can't tell me what connections to make. Sadly, this also means I can't tell Beep and her Beep-brain what connections to make. It is a shame. If I could just get in there and rearrange things, it would be quite healthy for her.

Rising to bait her, I ask, "Why were you out there? It's early for you."

She follows my stalking path across the room. "Couldn't stop thinking about last night. I figured you'd be the same."

I stop to sit in an imaginary therapy chair and grab an imaginary notebook. "And what makes you think that?"

"I know how much you want to find something better than hanging out here, stuck with me," Beep says. "And I know you thought what we saw last night could be it for you. I want you to have that, too."

I toss down the notes. "Don't lie. You want me here forever. You need me to bully you."

"I do." She nods. "I deserve it."

Thinking we might be on the verge of a breakthrough, I ask, "Why?"

"You think you know so much, and you don't know *that*?"

I wonder if it is Beep who is gay for me and terrified to admit it, but I play dumb. "Knowing more than you doesn't mean knowing everything. I could make something up... if you like."

She shakes her money-making mop-top, no. "I used to try to tell you, but I gave up. Maybe you'll figure it out. I just hope I'm not there when you do."

I bundle my knees and rock. "Intriguing, Beep, intriguing."

She changes the subject. "We should try to find out what happened to him."

Assuming she's talking alien, I say, "*It*. We should try to find out what happened to it."

"Fine." She gives it another extended fuck-you f. "It. You might be right. It could be something better for you."

Petty and petulant, I correct her again. "*Ick*. Ick could be something better." Then I catch myself. "Shit. Now I've gone and named it. But, as you said, how can we be sure all that happened, that it wasn't some midsummer night's dream?"

"There was nothing on the news, but..."

I don't have to see her satisfied smile. I feel it. She presents a screen for me to read.

"Hold the phone," I say.

"I know, right? The original post was deleted. This is a screen grab."

"No, I mean hold the phone steady. I can't read it with you waving it around like that."

She does. It's a social post from a young buck deputy, cock-bragging about a peculiar, pulpy prisoner found in the woods near Lincoln Way. He likewise wonders why the story isn't all over the news. Animal, vegetable or mineral, said captive is currently in our local jail, where they're trying to get it picked up by the feds. They were still waiting at the time of the post, an hour ago.

I question how/why Beep knows this man. Great as it would be to think she cultivates sources in anticipation of strange days like these, I find it disturbing that she does anything without my knowledge.

Her face tells me nothing. Her lips ask, "So, are we going to go find... ick?"

"No, Beep. *I* will go find ick. You will drive."

I'll be damned if I risk *my* learner's permit.

# 4

O h, the cleverness that is me.
     Not everyone can convince an unlicensed driver to steal their parents' car. With Mama and Papa Beep vacating for a few days, all it takes is the vague promise that we'll be back by nightfall. Next thing you know, Beep grabs the keys to the kingdom from a kitchen peg.

As victories go, this one's suspicious. As she starts that mother up, I can't shake the feeling she'd have offered the GTA without any cajoling from me at all.

Which means what? That she wants to get rid of me? Shunt me off into ET's arms because she's as sick of my presence as I am of hers? Such suppositions would threaten to upend my sense of superiority, were they not prima facie absurd. Given the rolling eye-candy that I am, Beep couldn't possibly want to get rid of me.

More likely, she does it, as she said, *for* me, her devotion fanatic to the point of lunacy. This, on the other hand, upends my sense of safety. Is she stalker-crazy?

Granted, when it comes to mental health, your humble navigator is hardly in a position to throw stones. Did I mention I was diagnosed schizophrenic?

At least, that's what the voices told me.

Whether I'm nuts, or, as I prefer to see it, the only sane one, isn't the collector's item here. Oh, I *get* the concerns; like, Shelley, if you're crazy, how do you know what's real? How do you know *anything's* real, Shelley? How do you know *everything's* not an illusion, Shelley?

First off, who said we were on a first name basis? Second,

the idea that everything's an illusion is total bullshit, fertilizer without a field, crap sans crop. Why? Because having a concept of illusion requires a concept of reality. Without that distinction, as in *everything* is one or the other, both are meaningless. Ergo, unless, or until shown otherwise, whatever's right in front of you, or sneaking up behind you, is real.

That's it. You can only play the cards you've been dealt.

Since we are here, let's talk about that other shambling, putrescent shibboleth; If a tree falls in the forest and no one's there to hear it, does it make a sound? Yes.

How do I know? The same way you know there's a tree falling in a forest and no one's there to hear it. And don't give me that evasive crap about how you can imagine a tree falling in a forest. If you can imagine a tree falling, I get to imagine it making a sound.

The real puzzle is how all the maladapts who came up with this garbage (and I include myself) survived this long. You'd think such a lineage, full of solipsistic anxieties, hollow elitism, asthma and allergies, real or metaphorical, would've died off long ago. That at the very least, we'd have all been tricked into a fake game of hide-and-seek, so that while we're counting ten, those who do the real work could sneak off and, ready or not, leave us to starve.

Somehow, we who wheezed when harvest came, or sneezed while tracking prey, convinced those with surplus food that we are worth the trouble. How? By asking if life is but a dream, imagining treefalls in soundless forests, pretending to read destiny in the stars, or otherwise feigning understandings that, even if they didn't bring advantage to the mighty, at least made them laugh and/or cry.

And we're doing it still.

Sure, *we* call it magic. Some of us go as far as to convince ourselves we have innate value—that winning the Internet is a thing. Deep down, though, we know damn well it's only branding. Push comes to shove, and everyone's again eating only thanks to the sweat on their brows and the dirt under their nails, we, the creators and custodians of idea and dream, will be the first to go.

Because, no, the rest of you do not *need* us to live.

No more than a rock needs meaning to be.

Yes, with our dying, wheezing breath, we will sneer and say, "You call *that* living?"

But we'll still taste like chicken, so you don't have to.

In these non-subsistence days, with so many free to puzzle over the notion that food originates somewhere beyond the fridge (you mean, there's a supermarket?) it's repulsively easy to think otherwise. Easier still if you find a self-affirming echo chamber, where, if you show the tribe your iambic pentameter, quote Wittgenstein or name the correct STOS episode, they'll worship you as a god.

A funhouse mirror version of a god, but a god, nonetheless.

To be clear, I did not come to this view of reality by choice. I did everything possible to avoid it. Craving that like hive-mind, I sought my people in the dingy backs of HS lunchrooms, comic stores, cons, LARPs, online gaming, worldwide domination chatrooms, and yes, through that ugly cosplay incident of which we shall speak no more. Time was, and what a time it was, I was so lonesome, I took some comfort there. Ultimately, familiarity breeds, and by virtue of that contempt, I rejected them all.

As astronaut Taylor says in Serling's original *Planet of the Apes* script, I can't help thinking that somewhere in the universe there has to be something better than [sic] man. Has to be. Yes, I know how it worked out for *damn you all to hell* Taylor, but you can't blame a girl for trying.

This is why, as sweet Beep sussed, finding and relating to an ick such as ick calls so deeply. However long it lasts, 't would be, for me, the intersection of genre and singularity, of narrative and happenstance, of world and idea, a screeching collision of expectation and occurrence, the fulfillment of will and its destruction. *Real* magic.

Once the thought occurs that magic might be real, how could anyone let it go?

Meanwhile, back in the moment, we're en route to the jailhouse on the edge of forever.

Blear itself isn't as small as it is empty; wide green spaces fill the gaps between buildings. You never *see* maintenance workers trimming those trees, but it gets done. The few strip-malls are a horn-dog cross-breed of failed past and abandoned future. Sleek windowed walls of failing cyber-entrepreneurs sit beside grungy Bait & Tackle shops. Dollar stores neighbor overprivileged spas. And there is one, just *one* Starbucks. This town is a hospice, where the throw-away cultures of sundry decades gather to die.

It *was* the economy, stupid, once upon a time.

Now? I've no idea how anyone makes money.

Rather than a sister town, Blear's chief rival is nature. Between flash floods, record-breaking High and Lois temps, a hurricane streaming season extended to a full ten episodes, the new Dark Age feels deliciously close.

Every quarter mile brings a plethora of more reasons to stick my thumb into ick and try to hitch a ride. Will there be obstacles? Of course. First, ick is in jail. Second, ick didn't seem to like me very much. The list goes on. Still, the longest infection begins with but a single strep.

The police? The least of my concerns, for Beep and I are dangerous women. Our savage wiles honed by eons of evolution, we are possessed by a boundless teen desperation.

Still, *some* sort of plan seems in order, to help us boldly go.

"How well do you know this deputy?"

The Beep-face scrunches. "I don't know him. I just follow his posts."

"Cyber-stalking, eh?" Though indiscernible to the naked eye, my opinion of her notches up. "Pray tell why this particular prey?"

A thin shrug of narrow shoulders. "I think he's funny."

Funny's a funny word, almost as bad as *there*. I consider glaring for more, but, subtext be damned, this is too far beyond our breaking and entering capers to risk Beep understanding my facial expressions. Hunting ghosts/selves had only a slim chance of piercing the veil. What's ahead has more definite cosmic implications, not to mention the possibility of jail time. Plus, spell things out now, when mistakes are made, I can say, "It was her."

"Do you mean funny like a stand-up, or funny in the self-destructive way he releases top secret information that could cost him his reputation and his job?"

"Both."

"Clarity, please. I'm not trying to shield you from a potential abuser. Some things only experience can teach. I want to know, for instance, if he could recognize us, in person or on, say, security cameras."

"Recognize *us*...?" Her voice happy-trails off. "No. He couldn't."

Bad enough I have to trust her screen-grab, now I'm relying on her conclusions. Still, she looks so semi-adult cute behind the wheel, squinting at the morning sun, wearing that torn T-shirt I gave her because I didn't want to wash it. Seeing her there, like that, me here like this, how can I stay angry? I mean, I'd like to, but I can't. ADD or bipolar? You decide. Either way, I find my concern melting into an unusual fondness.

"Ah, Beep," I say with a smile.

Okay, yes, maybe I do want to fuck her. Right now, anyway. Back when I said I didn't? I didn't. Sexuality is as fluid as gender. (Though gender-fluid sounds like something you'd have a hard time washing off your hands. Like ick.)

Not that I've changed my mind about dumping her ass ASA-Post-road-test. More like when I kiss her goodbye, it may be wet and sloppy.

It's too late for a plan anyway. The rolling green landfill hill hosting the Blear PD rises like Olympus above the Serengeti. No, Toto, not at all. Our view from below is the opposite of inspirational, naught but a flagpole and the tippy-top of a single-story roof.

My haute chauffeur signals a turn into the PD lot, forcing me to intervene. "No! Bad, Beep! Stick to the street."

"What? Why?"

"Up there be cameras. Obey me, Beep. I am not a harsh mistress."

Choosing from a score of empty spots, she centers the car between them. At least, if caught, a parking ticket won't be added to the list of charges.

No one is around. No one. It still being a lazy early morn, this lack of visible peeps would be normal—were it not for a certain spacecraft crash the night before.

I ask myself. "I get that the full fathom Deep State would keep an alien all hush-hush, but shouldn't there be *some* activity?"

Beep answers. "Maybe the post was a joke?"

If a Beep speaks in a forest and I don't care to hear her, does she make a sound?

With great benevolence, I explain. "Mind the logic gap. Can't joke about something no one should know about. Who's your audience?"

She tries to recover. "Disinformation?"

"Nonsense," I tell her.

She may be in the ballpark, though. It could be bait.

There could have been viddy last night. If cam-snagged, facial recognition would beget names, names beget online activity, online activity beget Beep's social following of a certain young buck deputy. Perhaps the disappearing post was a way to lure their only witnesses.

Why not pick us up at home? It so happens I've already made up an answer for that. If they took us for a couple of wild and crazy teens, hepped up on doobies, who lack the capacity to convince anyone of anything, they may only want to see if we're still paying attention. If *we* let it go, the Deep-but-not-profound State may do the same for us. The post, then, was a first and final offer to leave things well enough alone.

Imagining my importance again? It is a hobby, but learning that you're in a world where real aliens really crash puts *everything* up for grabs, no? And everything would include the possibility of being down if we show our recognized facials.

No. The hungry argument eats itself. To say anything about *everything* is life-is-but-a-dream territory. Truth is, we have no way of knowing what to expect. While not knowing may be uncomfortable, it is perhaps the most legit state of being.

*To let understanding stop at what cannot be understood is a high attainment,* said Zhuangzi, the Chinese philosopher who dreamed he was a butterfly, or maybe he was a butterfly who dreamed he was a... never mind. Point being, those who cannot let understanding stop when it should, will be destroyed on the lathe of heaven, by Ursula K. Le Guin. Rather than dangle a cruel illusion of agency, I don't tell Beep any of this.

Instead, I say, "Pretend to jog with me."

We trot, bods bouncing, like we're taking good care of ourselves for any male who might be gazing. A veer puts us in the slanted tree patch that separates the PD property line from a wholesome baseball field. Tree-patch is hyperbole. It's more like a comb-over to conceal the scant, balding foliage. Nothing like our prior garbage-strewn climb, we top the thirty-degree slant and drop.

A halfling-hedge provides cover for our peeping. I again expect a hubbub, a scene rife with, at least, meaning, but all's still quiet on the wasted front. The mute brick building calls to mind a toy-train model. The smeary-cloud sky, too silent to be real, resembles a painted canvas. Throw a rock hard enough, it'll hit eternity and come bouncing back.

Nearing the visitor's lot, the silence speaks volumes. No less than a dozen vehicles lay about like pieces in a losing game of Tetris. A few driver-doors are open wide, keys in ignitions, as if the occupants were rushing out when—oops—the Rapture occurred.

In for a penny-pound, we make for the entrance, heads bobbing to glimpse beyond the twin glass doors. Beep's attention on everything but her feet, she hits the auto-pad. When the doors slide open, she nearly jumps out of her skin.

I half-expect her to say, "Jinkies!"

Instead, she looks as annoyed with herself as I am. Inside we spy, with our little eyes, an empty waiting room and untended front desk. No movement, but there's sound now—ringing phones. Not just old-style jingle jangles, pre-recorded tones of all sorts, buzzing and farting from places unseen and no one's picking up.

It's like my dream a hundred times over.

Behind the reception counter, a particularly foreboding door is half-open. Even a species bad at sound location can tell most of the noise originates on the other side. It's not just any door. This is a manly door, the kind of portal so protective, you have to be buzzed through, the sort that should be open *or* closed, not wishy-washy undecided.

At counter's end we see the reason for this ambivalence; a body blocking the way. It's Beep's pal, young buck Deputy Dog. Though I draw no connection to the phone vibrating in his motionless hand, his pants are off.

Beep, closer than expected, says, "Not dead. Breathing."

The area buck's bod has left unsecure holds a yawn-boring collection of cubby-desks, all the seats cheap and empty. Which is not to say the room is empty, but it's easy to see why no one's answering their phones: Like the deputy, they're all down.

The weirdest of the weird? They've all been caught with their pants down. Not a metaphor, none of them have pants on. Oh, there are pants *around*; folded neatly, rolled inside out, hanging on chair-backs, stuffed in half-open drawers. None, though, are where'd you expect—*on* the legs of the men and women who paid perfectly good money for them.

Do they still wear shirts? Yes. Vests and jackets, too. Underpants and shoes? Apparently optional, but they've all got socks, *always* socks.

As if confirming we've stumbled upon the aftermath of an orgy, a pleased sigh issues forth from Deputy Dawg. I attempt to shield Beep's innocent eyes, but she snaps her head away.

"Have it your way," I say.

She does, kneeling, feeling for a pulse. She moves his collar, revealing, a bit of familiar ick against his neck.

She jumps back, but again does not say, "Jinkies!"

I touch it, but again, my sticky fingers do nothing for me.

The first happy groan belonged to Buck, but as we lean in close to one, then another, each time we hear pleasurable little sighs. Not quite coming from their lips, it's more akin to the way an ocean roars when you hold a conch to your ear.

Despite the plentiful bared bottoms, the overall ambience is more childlike than erotic. My sense is that this was not an orgy of the sex kind, but closer to the giddiness seen last night, a giddiness I am mysteriously unable to achieve. Not me, but maybe...?

I nod seductively twixt Beep and the goo. "Care to go

knock-knock-knockin' on the doors of perception?"

Beep goes all no-means-no. "Are you kidding?"

I eye the sighing bodies. "Don't you want to know why they look so happy?"

The mop-top head shakes with abandon. "Sometimes the dying look happy, too."

"Hmph. Point taken."

Disappointed to have my experiment thwarted by ethics, I move among the fallen. Unafraid of picking up something untoward, I quickly make my way toward the only other egress, labelled, conveniently, *Holding Cells*.

Beep, slow to follow, slower still to speak, slowly says, "Slow down."

I wave at the tone-filled air. "Au contraire, mon Beep. That's a lot of people calling. We'll have company soon."

Nodding agreement, she opens the door.

*Holding Cells* was a misnomer. There is only one, a singular cell, and yet I am far from dissatisfied by the deception. In it, to my everlasting joy, is both ick and ick. There's a bench in there as well, but ick does not sit upon it so much as pool.

Overeager, I approach. "We've come to help!"

Lo, miracle of miracles, ick responds, or at least gives off a few slime bubbles.

In order for my sense of self and the narrative to continue, here I must at least pretend ick has a face I've just seen, and that it does what faces do, at least in the sense of expressing inner states. I could be wrong. In terra incognita, it's possible the basic Me/Not Me distinction isn't universal.

Anyway, it burbles as if to say, "Wha?"

Rather than completely blow Beep's mind, I give only the vaguest gist of the great communique that has passed between myself and the alien mind:

"Ick wants to get out of here and come with us. I can feel it."

Speaking of faces, hers does major scrunching. "Please. You have *no* idea what it's thinking, or if it thinks at all."

Ick seems to blurp in agreement.

I ignore them both. "Pick him up."

"No!"

"Still afraid of tripping the light fantastic?"

"Same as I was two second ago. Yes."

"Then *I* will."

Another face-scrunch. "You can't!"

"No?"

Poor dear. I let her do so much for me, she's convinced herself I can do nothing at all. I enter the open cell, reach beneath the most solid bits of ick I can find and heft. Ick's no lightweight, but as the copious goo drips off, the load is more manageable.

Beep is aghast. "How?"

"The goop effects-me-not. I know not why."

More importantly, there is none of last night's resistance from our strange visitor. "Figured out who your friends are, eh, ick? That's all right, you don't have to answer. I'm just glad you're here."

As I maneuver ick outward, a fearful Beep keeps her distance, but does hold the door for us. To her further credit, when we reach an emergency exit, she doesn't hesitate to kick it open. The resulting alarm joins the ringtones in a noise-music band that we are happy to leave muffled by the closing door.

We're outside again, but in the employee lot, surrounded by last night's emergency vehicles. In the light of day, it's easy to see these puppies are military issue, but that hardly means the feds are involved. Po-po probably bought them at an *everyone-must-go* army surplus sale. Can't say I blame the officers for breaking out this gear, given that there weren't peaceful protestors involved. There is so very little to do in Blear.

Which brings another thought to mind: "Ick's pretty lucky to have landed near such a withered limb of the military industrial complex." Beep's nod most assuredly meaning I'm wrong, I hurry to change my mind. "Then again, that may have been ick's intent, a manifestation of alien agency."

Ick bubbles, as if to say, "No."

Before I can conjure another option, time's up. We have company.

None of that same old same movie/TV stuff. No SWAT teams, Black-OPs choppers, or roaring SUVs brimming with armed paramilitary. What we do get is the high-pitched whine of what the more racist among the Harley-Davison crowd call a rice grinder; a motorcycle engine, tuned for efficiency over noise, bite over bark.

As it comes into view, I have to ask myself, "How many times can you say *what the…* in a single 48-hour period?"

A motorcycle yes, but not in the usual two-wheeler sense. It's a motor-*uni*cycle, a single, spinning wheel with a dark-helmeted motorist neatly balanced up top. A real circus act, which, sadly, can never pop a wheelie.

Ere the motorist start juggling flaming bowling pins, or see us, we book ere we came. Carrying ick makes the effort less an elegant ballet of fleet-footed subterfuge and more a plodding mess of squishing sounds, but we make it to the semi-cover of the semi-trees. Thinking we're safe, I pause for a foolish look back and almost know how Lot's wife felt.

The newcomer has stopped. Helmet off, he sees us. I see him.

Something wordless passes between us, which, as usual, I will now put into words. At a glance, we realize this is kismet. No mere intruder in my dust, he is the veritable Yang to my Yin, the hensile to my prehensile, the phallus to my yoni.

And oh, what a dick he is.

The chiseled features beneath a bald-by-choice dome make the helmet aesthetically redundant. I can tell just by looking at that sweat-covered stubble that he wants to hunt me, not to hunt himself, but to get me, to hurt me, to bring me down in a primal, protozoan way. He believes in guns and knows how to use them, thinks Doctor Who should always be a man, James Bond white, that the civil war was fought over state rights, not slavery (all of them, including the one between Steve and Tony), and that the two-headed Obama/Hillary caused Climate Change by eating the arctic shelf.

For my part, I fight to contain a near-implacable desire to tell him why he should not eat hamburger, how the name of his football team is inherently racist, exactly which words he should not use, and that a drunk cannot provide consent, even if he's the only one drunk.

Instinct dies hard in those such as myself, who claim to use magic, but I'm too close to getting the ick out of here. So, for the sake of the reality I hold in my arms, I hold back. Besides, not everyone knows how right I am about everything. My righteous words, no matter how accurate, are truth-bombs likely to fall on deaf-dick ears.

So, we see Dick and run.

Run from Dick, run.

# 5

We're in the shit now, sliding down faint foliage to side-walk level. Lovable Beep dashes car-ways, eye-candy me galumphs behind, inscrutable ick hanging in my arms, dripping like a huge melting carton of water-flavored ice cream.

"Get back here!" Dick shouts from above.

"Like that's gonna work," I say with a girlish laugh.

We're halfway across the street when Dick's monocycle revs, whining something awful, single tire squealing. It occurs to me that while ordering our return was doomed to failure, chasing us could easily work. Especially if Dick has any weapons beyond his disarming personality.

Key in hand, Beep beep-unlocks the doors which should never have been locked. Crazy frantic, she accidentally beep-locks them before finally leaving them the beep-open.

The poor dear's all nerves, but she's fast, oh, how fast! I've barely got ick slopping in the driver-side backseat and she's got the car in gear. Unfortunately, *I* am not yet in. While never having leapt into a moving car, I have sat motionless for my fair share of action flicks. Virtually knowing better than to waste time circling round the hood, I dive in the back, atop my prize. Crawling through ick to reach shotgun, I suppress an urge to pat myself on the back for a job well done.

Car peeling as best a hybrid can, Beep nails her eyes on the road ahead and asks, "Do you see him?"

Part of me dreads looking, but I do. The news isn't all bad. Way, way, back, Dick's just now one-wheeling out the PD lot. Leaning our way to turn, he looks like a terribly irate circus clown.

"Take a turn, Beep, any turn! Take two! They're small."

She not only does, she gets compulsive about it, taking one turn after another, leaving none for the other guests. Together, they form an impressive zigzag pattern that lasts until Dick's either gone, or we're too dizzy to see him.

Engine rush aside, we indulge the relative quiet of our own heavy breathing, interrupted only by the occasional plop of whatever's oozing off ick and onto the upholstery.

"The seats!" Beep notices. "My parents will kill me!"

I eye ick, sitting, lying, whatever, there. Ick is either fine, or dead, it's hard to tell.

Deciding to be optimistic, I say, "I saved you, ick."

A gentle bloop-blort seems to answer: "Wait? What??"

Of course, it's only natural that ick, as any space explorer, would be full of questions. All those bubbles no doubt mean it's mission-focused, gathering data for its distant, longed-for home, selflessly seeking answers to the big questions, questions like:

"Who the fuck are you?" and "Oh God, oh God, what's happening to me?"

Perhaps that furious boiling is how they show gratitude on ick's world. I have so much to learn. Until then, I try to comfort my guest.

"I'd like to take you home with us," I say-sing. "I'd love to take you home."

Surprisingly, Beep's all over the fab salt-and-pepper reference. "I don't really want to stop the show, but, that's the first place they'll look."

A turn of my nose upwards. "Other thoughts, have we?"

A dizzy blonde shake of her brunette head. "Not sure. The state park?"

A tsk. "I wasn't talking to you, Beep. I was talking to myself."

A snippy, "As usual."

Apparently, there are no sheep in foxholes. I endeavor to explain. "Speaking to oneself *is* the best way to ensure an intelligent conversation, isn't it, ick?"

"Kill me, just kill me," comes the perhaps-imagined reply.

Where *do* we go from here? Wherever it is, we'll be followed, probably by more Dick than one. Given that, it should be a temporary refuge, easily abandoned. But isn't everything temporary, life itself loose change at best?

I wish there were a spot Blear-abouts with the proper ambience; an abandoned mental institution, an old factory where orphaned children were once made into Amazon products, or, to be more Shirley Jacksonian, a place where the walls continue upright, doors are sensibly shut, and whatever walks, walks alone. If there were, y'think I'd bother ghost-hunting in McMansions? Fuck, no.

Best we've got is an old iHop that was briefly converted to a strip joint before being oops-burnt for reassurance purposes. Fond as I am of syrup (and, all things ick-like) a charred blue roof across from an interstate rest stop does not make for a great hideout from the coppers.

As I think my thoughts, Beep sadly defaults to her own. Always a mistake, but by the time we reached the entrance to the aforementioned state park, I've still got nothing better.

"Fine. Get us up as high as you can, so we can see what's coming."

Ick gurgles and/or drips. Beep says something I'm sure she considers significant, but I don't, and so won't repeat. Lowering the window, I stick my head out, doglike, feeling the wind against my lolling tongue and the view against my eyes. Whose woods these are, I think I know; Garbage can, kiosks, bench, bench, bench. Picnic tables, rusty grills, bench, bench, bench.

I seem to remember a Bigfoot sighting here a decade ago, or was it Santa Claus? I always get hairy man-like brutes confused. It is remote, though, the dirt access road entrances and exits tough to spot—unless you spent your childhood hiking here, before the asthma kicked in. To be fair, I'm breathing stronger these days. At least I think I am. Can't remember my last attack.

She finds a spot, flat and full of grass, with a decent view of what's coming below and lots and lots of sky. Car doors shuck and click. We humans get on out.

Clasping hands behind head, Beep leans forward and, with small, but good, vibrations, tries to make her forehead touch her groin. It could be an effort to stretch, but she looks as if she's weeping.

I put my butt to the car. "The local yokels *must* have contacted the Powers That Be. So where are the pros? Why haven't they taken over?"

"Maybe…"

I finger-snap. "Alimentary my dear canal. Alien crash stories are easy to ignore. The sky-tracking people likely took it for a meteor, while the goo rendered the eye-witless babbling drunks at best. While such cray-cray may not keep the PTBs from checking it out eventually, it could make lower echelon MIBs less eager to respond, like, hey, let's grab a decent breakfast first before we drive all the way out to bumfuck Blear."

I expect a *brilliant, Holmes, you've done it again!*

I get an impertinent, "What about the guy on the unicycle?"

"What about him?"

"Why'd he chase us?"

"Because we're cute?"

She looks up from her bend. "Seriously?"

Apparently, my congrats is getting further away. "Come on, Beep, there are holes in any argument, some more holy than others. Might you be more impressed if I said I think I know why the goo has no effect upon me?"

She goes back down. "No."

"Could you at least pretend, then? Now, please?" I take the eye roll as a yes. "It's ick, right? So, it's under ick's domain. Sensing our commonality, ick is protecting me."

She rises so quickly, something in her spine clicks into, or out of, place.

"Is *that* what you think? Shelley, you can't…"

Another trail voice, capped with another *fuck-you,* "Fine."

"There is *one* thing I don't understand. Pained as I am to say it, it's about you."

Warming to *any* attention, especially mine, she gives me the shiny eyes. Currently too occupied to be a complete sadist, I acquiesce. "Everyone who dares so much as approach the goo finds themselves enthralled, yet you haven't tried to touch it. Why?"

She parks her butt on the car, cozy-next to mine. Sun lower, all the world ablaze with light, she looks at her feet.

you go along. You keep piling one assumption on another, you could get lost in there."

She motions toward my head, making it clear exactly what she means by *in there.*

I sigh the saddest of sighs—for today. "Unless I start *somewhere,* I won't have anything to be wrong about, will I? Does my droogie have another suggestion? A tack for a room all your own?"

"Yes. Will you listen for a change?"

"Perhaps."

"Okay, then I suggest that, at least for now, there actually be a *we,* not just a you. If we both agree it's trying to say something, doesn't that improve the odds we're right?"

I want to tell the obvious child no, that such a vote would only improve the odds that we're talking to each other, something I'm dying to get away from. I want to make it clear it is I, and I alone, who should have my hand on the Ouija planchette.

My righteous anger is fruitless. There isn't time for things to keep spiraling like this. To regain control of the situation, I must regain control of myself. To regain control of myself, I must regain control of Beep. Recalling her concern about the car's interior, I offer a distraction:

"What say we get ick out of there and air him?"

A single headshake says, "Not touching it."

My narrowed eyes answer, "So much for a *we.* Et tu, *you?*"

She exhales, pops the trunk, removes a tarp, and lays it out like a picnic blanket.

Her crossed arms say, "That's my half. Your turn."

Struggling not to make faces, lest I sink any hope for a hasty return to the status quo, I go in deep. The backseat is a god-awful mess, one that can't possibly be cleaned or explained, but we'll probably die in a barrage of gunfire long before the issue comes up.

Wriggling my arms along Mr. Sloppy's glop, I get them under the solid bits and plop the newest member of our team onto the tarp for some tea, sympathy and interrogation.

"How do you do that?"

"Physics, B, physics. What's it going to be now, we? How do *we* speak with ick?"

"Not exactly." Maintaining a cautious distance, she kneels. "If it's a, what does a traveler want? To get to somewhere, or back from somewhere, right?"

Deciding not to mention that both amount to the same thing, I play along.

She waves a hand at the sky, pointing at one spot then another. "Is there someplace you want to get to, ick?"

The resulting plish-plop is loud and clear.

Over-excited, over-convinced, Beep points up. "Home?"

The plopping gets crazy, like splish-splash, ick's takin' a bath, long about a Saturday night. It's got a beat, and it's fun to dance to, but I give it a four.

"No, Beep," says I. "He who wanders isn't necessarily lost. Those bubbles are mere coincidence, utterly unlike the richly textured messages *I* receive."

Her slack open mouth makes a frustrated sound. Comes next the shouting: "This is what I'm talking about! Do you want to communicate with an alien intelligence or just pretend? Because if you want to pretend, we may as well go home and use my Barbies!"

"Heavens. I'm trying to ensure that we're *not* playing Barbies."

She points up again, nodding like a bobble. "Home? Yes?"

"Beep, please. Trust me, the Great ick is not going to respond to such a…"

For the first time, ick moves. Like a larva attempting to birth itself, ick props ick-self up on those brittle, wobbly hard parts, and makes a noise just like… well, what's the opposite of silent, but deadly?

It's the second miracle of the day. First alien contact. Now, Beep is right about something. Overwhelmed by the flatulence, I blurt:

"If I help you get back, will you take me with you, ick?"

The limb-things lose it. The amazing alien slumps into a whimpering puddle.

Beep says, "I think that means, no." A pause, then, "You want to leave the planet? You think that's a good idea?"

I know I agreed to this tag-team talk, but it's gone too far.

Buzzkill Beep is the problem. I'm *not* projecting too much of myself, I'm projecting too little. If I'm to be understood, to grok ick and have ick grok me, I have to get rid of her.

But that's not what's worrying me. It's how to do it. These things must be done delicately, or you hurt the spell.

Besides, she has the car keys.

# 6

To re-Beep: *Do* I want to leave the planet? Of course. Have you seen the rent?

No doubt some cry foul—a teen girl from Podunk would never read *Gravity's Rainbow* let alone leave it all behind. Such Neander-thralls rank with the medieval priests who executed children for speaking Latin. How could an uneducated girl know so much, without a devil's help? Never mind she attended Mass every Sunday and has ears and brain—demons must be speaking through her! Burn, witch, burn!

Fact is, in our internet daze, you have *no idea* what anyone should or should not know. Tree of Knowledge? Ha! We live in an orchard, and the incognizanti let themselves starve. As for me, well, what was the name of the prophet who could see things so very clearly, but was condemned never to be believed? Cassandra. A better name than Shelley, but not by much.

For those with ears to hear, I'll try, best as I can, to carry on.

Why seek to leave this torrid terra firma, its oppression and stupidity aside? Same reason I hunt ghosts, aliens, selves, et al: to find the words that will take my heart, fully and truly scrumptious, perfect and whole, across the placeless void and into the sanctity of someone else's head. Could be your head, I don't know. That part doesn't matter.

It's the Holy Grail we of the useless tribe have desperately attempted for millennia, only to encounter the same stubborn wall. Yes, Terence said: *I am human, therefore nothing human is alien to me,* but the species-wide hug has darker corollaries: Being human, I can only see *as* a human, unable to understand what it *is* to be human any more than a fish understands water, until they're suffocating in the air.

To truly see self *requires* the alien. Only outside looking in can I actually say you, say me, say it for always, the way it should be. Without that, you are as much ick to me as ick, and ick as much you.

Can't get there from here, you say? Once you cross a boundary, the new terrain becomes part of human experience and therefore no longer alien? Sure, in terms of the binary Before and After, but in-between there's a moment *as* you breach, when all is one and one is all, when truth is not only accessible, but communicable. Like a disease.

Does that mean if I get there, that you, or anyone, will catch it? Maybe, but the likelihood remains, tragically delicious, that no one will understand. The things most sacred and personal always run the risk of being taken for gibberish. To be completely honest, if you do somehow understand my secret sweet-spot words, and I get on in there to mingle in your mind, I'd probably hang out half a minute, make a nasty comment about your décor, then want, with equal frenzy, to be anywhere else but in your head.

In the end, even brain cells die alone.

That wouldn't be as bad as failing, though. After all, does a transitory nature make something less worthwhile, or more? I say more. Souls unchanging and eternal are worthless. The only river with value is the one I put my foot in but once. Reality moves. To be in touch with it, the mind must also move.

Beep, though, has got to go.

"We need supplies," I tell her. "Drive to a store and come back later."

Her mien gets mangles. "Supplies? What kind of supplies? For what?"

To further annoy her, I mirror her face. "You'll think of something. Start with better flashlights."

She protests. "But... you think you can stay here without me?"

"Of course."

She huffs and puffs as she enters the car. The car does

likewise as she drives off, her Beep sounds fading beneath the slurps and sloshing of ick. Not completely impervious to the feelings of lesser beings, I experience a fading regret. Should I have warned her not to use her phone or credit card? Aside from the high data/interest rates, they can be tracked.

Beep, who, among fools is no fool, must know that, right?

Let it go, let it go. Plot points are always antithetical to the moment. Besides, I am alone with ick at last. Seeking proximity, I kneel into the goo. I try to seem pleasant, but fear I lost the knack long ago.

"She's gone, ick. Is there anything you want to tell me now that she's not here?"

After a thoughtful beat, there is a sensation for which I provide words:

"No. What made you think there was?"

Unacceptable. That can't be ick. I must be projecting, and I, as ick, must be lying to me. There's a further truth to be had here, and I will chase it round Perdition's flames before I give it up!

I try another tack. "Can you grant me a wish?"

"What? No."

I splay my knees, wetting legs and jeans to bring myself closer. "Work with me, ick. Can you at least cough up some incredible alien secret?"

The burbles acquire a different ambience, less rambunctious fart, more aquarium aerator.

"Secret? Like what?"

I'm not *completely* certain the answer's entirely mine. Well, well, well. Doing what I do best, I work harder at being myself.

"If I knew what kind of secret I wanted, it wouldn't be secret, would it? Something aliens know, but humans don't, because you're all superior and beyond us."

"Do you hear yourself?"

Hearing something I'd clearly say to Beep throws it all in doubt again. Yet, if it *is* just me chatting myself up, I can't imagine why I'd treat myself like Beep. I *like* me. The ambivalence leaves me wrapped in strange sin. I am not I, yet I am not pretending.

I play the cards I've felt. "I'll spell it out for you, ick, I'm

talking the meaning of life, of me, and I don't mean 42. I want
to know myself, as was inscribed atop the Temple at Delphi.
Not *know myself* in the biblical sense, of course, but... scratch
that. Not *necessarily* in the biblical sense, I am quite the catch."

The reaction is... *very* different. Beneath the blorps and
flerches of both the goo and my own humming mind, I *do* hear
a voice, one that gets under the language the way Janis Joplin's
voice gets under the melody, a voice too free of dirt and signal
noise to be entirely of this world or mine.

"You? Why would you want to know what you are?" it says.

Ouch. Okay, then. Never said it would be painless.

I try for sincerity: "Because I do. I do want to know. Can
you tell me?"

There's a pause, perhaps to ponder the best response, but
this voice is far too new for me guess what its silence means.

Hope-filled as I am, my faith is horrifyingly fragile. A few
seconds of quiet is all it takes to sink my battleship. I fill with
dread that what I thought a lifeline thread is gone forever, a
wisp ended before I could grasp it. Yet just before my wreckage
hits bottom, an answer comes:

"Maybe. In a way."

I grin, a Cheshire fool, as besotted with believing as I was
drowned with doubt. A starry-eyed tippler, I lie on the tarp,
spooning my soft, yet callous creature.

"Then I'll help you, ick! No matter what it takes, or where
it takes us!"

"I didn't ask for your help."

"You didn't have to, ick, you didn't have to." I wipe away a
tear, or a bit of goo. "We have a deal now."

Am I sure I can deliver unto ick, or that ick will deliver
unto me? No, but that impossible world in which I might truly
live, is now, at least possible.

I roll onto my back beside my nascent lover and sigh. A
calmness takes me. Looking up I try to attend whatever the
massive sky above might tell me. Not much, it turns out. Blue
and white with cool air is all it has to say. It's all good. Let the
celestial Jack Benny vault be as numb and stupid as the insect
brains that dwell beneath it.

It matters not, for ick and I have a deal.

As a result, I'm not so terribly annoyed to see Beep upon her return, some twenty minutes later. She emerges from the car, junk-food laden, not a flashlight in sight, but I can't say I mind at all.

"Hello," I say. For a change, I mean it.

"Hello?" she says back, uncertain.

She's already sensed the difference in me. It confuses her, making the most basic communication between us suspect. My smile confuses her all the more.

I should tell her, all of it.

On second thought, no. It's mine and I want to keep it. But I certainly deserve credit for considering the option. If there were only some way to convey my moral worth to Beep without also explaining why. I *do* have to convey some version of the truth, one compelling enough to enlist her aid in getting ick wherever ick needs to go. Much as it pains me, telling her she was right about ick wanting to go home could provide enough Beep-glee to keep her from getting too curious.

I'm thinking about how best to phrase it, wondering if I should have ick tell her, through me, of course—but there's no time for any of that.

I hear we are not alone.

Has Dick and his helmeted burrowing head found us? No. This is based purely on a childlike genre conviction that we are fated, star-crossed nemeses. It's not him. The sound is all wrong for monocycle man, too loud, too fulsome, too variegated.

I sit up fast. The resulting slurp of back-leaving-goo briefly drowns the distant engines, but their distance does not last. Remember those cliché SWAT teams, Black-OP choppers and roaring SUVs bearing paramilitary troops I mentioned earlier? It's them.

"Beep! Did you use a credit card?"

As choppers rise in unison over the tree line, there is terror on her face.

"Debit, why?"

I can't believe it, yet I must, because it's true. No matter how stereotypically stupid things become, reality is not the aberration. It can't be.

It's the ideas we have about it that are always, always wrong.

# 7

It's not *just* like on TV. At best, the once-glass teat can only spew isolated narrative peaks. Screens, large or small, leave out many things, like the taste of dirt and leaf swept mouthward by the whipping chopper blades. Likewise, when you think you may actually die, the adrenaline rush isn't nearly as tame. Far from a child enjoying a free-wheeling roller-coaster action-movie ride, my telltale heart is much more a prisoner yanking iron-heavy bars.

Still, we're not so different from our screens. Our vaunted brains forever filter a billion streaming sensations, leaving only the one or two that will best allow continued survival. Under threat, the great globe itself, and all which it inherit, dwindles into a few quick, animal questions that beg for a thoughtless response.

Car or woods? Car.

Wrong answer.

Oh, we make it into the auto, ick and all, and Beep does peel on out, but from there we only get far enough to do a near head-on with the arriving armada of SUVs. She tries to swerve left, to get around them, but, acting on some whim I've confused for instinct, I scream:

"Go right! Now!"

I don't know why I screeched that, beyond a knee-jerk assumption that whatever direction I pick would have to better, because I'm me, but as the wee hybrid flies off-road and down, it doesn't seem the right choice at all.

We bump a boulder that would've stopped us cold were it not for momentum forcing us over the top. The rattling impact wreaks havoc with the undercarriage. She'll need a new muffler at least, yet the wheels and drive train remain intact, allowing us to roll, merrily, along.

Or maybe *careen* would be a better word.

We've spent a lot of time on tree-filled hills lately, this being our third, but that hardly explains how the speeding car manages to avoid the many tall, stiff pines that flaunt their wood every which way but loose. Turns out there is an explanation—it doesn't.

We slam a tree-trunk, thinner than most, most only proving it's not the size of the wand but the damage it performs. The hybrid front-end folds like a hurdy-gurdy (barrel organ, not wheel fiddle), while we, in full compliance with the laws of physics, shuck forward.

And ick? Some days, you're the alien intelligence, some days, you're the bug.

Goo splatters the windshield. Airbags belch, not unlike that weird, roly-poly uncle you were left alone with that one time, and ohgodohgodohgod, offer a violent, body-crunching hug.

Once motionless, I feel entitled to a brief silence, but the droning of the chase scene shit-show disallows a moment's peace. Not sure where the SUVs have gotten themselves to, but the choppers hover above. Unable to land for the trees, they shed black-jacketed troops, who fast-rope like hungry baby spiders diving out of an egg-sac sun.

I scream: "Not *that* right, Beep! The other one!"

Buried beneath a bubblegum butt bag, she says, perhaps to me, "Asshole."

A bruise wells on the bridge of her wee pixie nose.

"Could be worse," I say. "We could be in Philadelphia."

Prying ick from the glass to my arms, I exit. There is considerably less goo, but a gurgling assures me the good parts remain.

Lest Beep follow, I shout: "Throw yourself on their mercy! Blame me! You can still get yourself out of this."

She goes all potty-mouth. "Fuck you and your bullshit. You just want to use me as a distraction to give you a better chance at getting away!"

"Things *can* have more than one purpose," I explain.

If she replies, I don't hear it. Given the roar of the greasepaint and the smell of the crowds, she'd have to be louder. I fling my body eclectic, launching into a running downhill-fall kind of thing. Unfortunately, events vote in favor of falling, a slippery slope that quickly morphs into a fascist fetal-ball roll.

Tumbling round and round, wet leaves against back, ick on my front, I land in a generous ditch astride a dirt road. It being the road leading to our hilltop, the SUVs will be motoring down it, any second now.

There is, I admit, nowhere left to run.

There is also, however, a van waiting.

No, really, a van.

Painted a psychedelic Day-Glo Scooby-Doo, I trust it not in the least. Would you?

Beep arrives, but before I can tell her to call an Uber, the door slides open. The woman inside is pale enough to warrant avoiding eye contact. Her lean, muscled form is not so much mesmerizing lesbian-vampire as it is addict about to beg for change.

A hand is offered. Hers, not mine. To Beep, not me.

"Us or them," Handy-girl says. "Now, or never."

Saviors are hard to come by, but this one comes bearing pinned eyes, raggedy clothes and a lifespan shortened by self-abuse. Still, her unknown intent is potentially better than that of our gun-wielding pursuers.

I try to hop in, but don't make it.

With a sort of irritated street-tough grunt, Handy-girl makes a grab for my ick, but no way is that gonna happen. Arms locked, I hop again, this time landing sideways in the seat-less cabin, floored, but in full possession of my possessions.

Ignoring bruised-nose Beep's enjoinder to 'give me a sec', Handy-girl goes for the door. A breathless hope rises that the Beep-less part of my life will finally begin, but, my perky girl-pal dives in right before the door slides shut.

Windows black save for the windshield, all I get is a backside view of the front bucket seats. I do know HG isn't driving, because pedal to the metal, the van lurches forward. Anything not held down, including myself, ick and Beep, slide-sail to the rear. I expect Handy-girl to join us, but she strap-hangs by the door, drunk-smiling at us like she's finally found someone she can feel superior to.

"Debit card?" Handy-girl says.

Still potty-mouth angry, Beep answers: "Guess I forgot I was in a fucking action movie."

HG does not care for this. "Oh? What part of the fucking movie comes next? The part where you shit your pants, get all weepy and say you're sorry for giving me attitude?"

Under other circumstances, I might defend Beep, she being *my* idiot, but there's too much else demanding my attention. Specifically, the gun Handy-girl pulls from the small of her back.

It's either too heavy for her wimp-limp wrist, or she's more stoned than she looks, which is saying something. It flops about in a way that makes her look more fool than cool. Dangerous fool, though. Feeding on Beep's increasing terror, she goes in for a second helping.

"Or maybe I shoot you and throw you out of the van? You want that part to come next?"

Beep audibly tightens her sphincter. "No, please."

Handy-girl's disappointed pout makes me wonder if we'd have been better off entertaining the troops. At least then we'd be dealing with institutional stupidity, rather than this more individualized cray-cray.

Speaking of the military industrial Freudian complex, I'm surprised they haven't run us down already. The helicopters chuff like a horde of giant weed-whackers, as if ready to shred the roof, but then a sharp left turn flops us all to the right, and the unpainted windshield goes dark.

Judging from the coquettish hint of rounded concrete ceiling, we've entered an awfully convenient tunnel. I'm guessing storm-drain thing, rather than secret evil HQ. In support of the former, we bump and swish through shallow water, until, yea, verily, before us appears the veritable light at the end of the tunnel.

The choppers reduced to ambient noise, we crunchy-stop

on gravel, not quite emerging into the fullness of day, thanks to some natural overhang.

Curiouser and curiouser.

There are three more vans here, making for a jolly foursome. Two are painted to match our Hanna-Barbera travesty, but the other is so vanilla you could easily lose it in a parking lot because there are so many others like it. Perhaps that's the point.

Wait. My mistake on the foursome. There's a fifth wheel, and I do mean *wheel*, sleek and black and leaning against a utility pole. It's a monocycle.

Which means... Dick!

A quick sideways glance at our driver confirms his phallic bald-head identity.

I *knew* it! I *knew* we'd be nemeses! Sure, it's one of those clichés I claim to dread, but who wouldn't be tickled by such a blatant affirmation of gut instinct?

Any port in a storm, eh, Moriarty?

Before I can compose some clever way to acknowledge him, Dick exits, his place at the wheel taken over by another, far less interesting street-type. Yanking open the slider, Handy-girl gun-herds us out. The triplet of Mystery-mobiles go their separate ways. Looking like an Xmas stocking-stuffer for girls who've been bad, Dick waves us into his non-descript van.

"Could've saved us both a *lot* of trouble if you'd just stopped back in town."

New genre, new expectations. Heroes now, we hunt the villains and ourselves, and all must play their roles. I aim my chin at the departing Scooby vans.

"Nice distraction, unless they're tracking with heat-seeking x-ray drones."

"Are you crazy?" Beep says to our captors. "That was an army! They're going to find you."

Darling Dick's eye-roll begins with a nice arrogance, true, but the hesitancy undermines it, making me think I've made him worry that there *are* x-ray drones tracking us.

"Psh. Stupid." He whistles us in.

Not much on rejoinders, granted, but I can work with it. At least this time there are seats and an air conditioner. Beep, ick and I settle in our second-row seats. Handy-girl takes shotgun. Given the handgun, it's a bit of a misnomer. Outside, Dick sways in a gloriously ape-like fashion as he loads the monocycle in the van's spacious cargo area.

By the time he's behind the wheel, I'm ready for banter: "You buy all those vans just for little old us?"

Beep repeats, "They're going to find us."

He pulls leisurely onto the road. "Don't think so. I've been using those decoys to fuck with the state police for years and never lost any merchandise. No reason to think they won't work now."

My wheels turn with the van's. "Merchandise meaning drugs."

Beep makes a pained sound. "A dealer?"

"Like on the street? Nah. More like middle management with executive potential." He's not so much offended as trying to show off.

To better show off myself, I'm about to fill in the blanks, but Beep ruins it by popping the question, "Then... what do you want with an alien?"

"She means ick," I correct.

Fear restoring obedience, Beep capitulates. "I mean ick."

Dick goes frowny. "Ick?"

Ick blorbles, as if to say, "My name's not ick."

"Hold up." Cautious as Dick is, he's having trouble staying in his lane. "You think that gunk can think, that it's alive? It's that why you're running around with it, like you're doing an ET thing?"

"Duh, Dick, duh," I say. "Though, as a woman, I'm thinking more *Arrival*, with Amy Adams, or *Contact* with Jodie Foster."

Head slow-shaking, as if he's wise, Dick laughs a contemptuous little laugh. "I thought *I* was high."

Beep asks the obvious. "If you *don't* think it's alive, why...?"

Here it is, my chance to play Holmes, because I know the answer, I swear I do, it's on the tip of my tongue. But adrenaline's got that damn Beep-brain working overtime, so she stupidly answers her own stupid question, because she's stupid, stupid, stupid.

"Drugs. Alien designer drugs."

Dick does a trigger-finger-shooty thing, synchronized with a sharp tongue-click, to show his approval. "Yep. Got a get a text from my po-po boy about that shit last night, only then, I get more texts that're like increasingly batshit. Dude barely finished high school, and he's talking about his mask dripping off into reality, how everybody's mind is open and…"

Beep and I respond simultaneously. "…they start taking off their pants?"

He lights up like we're bonding over a show we binge-watched. "Right? I mean, wow. Look, all I want to do is snag some of that snot and get it to one of my chemists for, you know, deformulation, so I can get it to market. When I saw you running off, I thought you were the competition. Got your name off the PD system, popped it into an app, and waited until that debit card came up." Another laugh. "But it's cool, you're no threat, just up to your panties in some fucked up LARP shit."

Dick doesn't care about me? About ick? About LARPs? My irritation no longer knowing where to begin, I'm about to say something that will likely get us both killed. But ick and I have a deal. Rather than actualize our deaths, I deign lower my voice and lean into buddy-Beep for a hiss.

"They seem to like you better. Ask Heisenberg why he didn't just take a sample back at the station. That place was dripping like the walls of Caligula's bedroom."

She does, in her own simple way.

The question throws him all the same. "Sample what? The place was bone dry." A frown. A look at Handy-girl. "Scoop some of that shit."

Living up to her nickname, Handy-girl whips some latex gloves and a wrapped-in-plastic jar from the glove compartment. Without so much as a *'may I?'* she twists back and proceeds to violate our cult of personal space. Ick bubbles in protest, but if it means being freed without further ado, I decide to stay put. Having gathered her goo, Handy-girl screws the lid back on, tight.

"Much as I've enjoyed our chat," I say, "We can go now, right?"

Beep face-presses the window. "Anyplace along here is fine."

A smirk. He slows. "Sure. I can use another decoy to keep them off my trail. You think you can outrun that fucking army, all power to you."

As Handy-girl raises the glass for closer inspection, the sample... what? Evaporates is the wrong word, since it means it turned into vapor. Without any in-between state, the sample disappears.

I look at ick. "Something you're not telling me?"

"Huh," Dick brilliantly observes. "That makes things complicated."

No shit. He can't let us go sample-free, at least not *with* ick.

As he gets back up to the speed limit, I give ick a shake, hoping against hope for a response along the lines of, "Kidding! I can fix you up a batch of everlasting goo that won't disappear easy as pie *and* give you the recipe! Here ya go. Drop us at the next corner, please."

No such luck. Like the singing amphibian in One Froggy Evening, ick remains motionless. Nor do any words appear in my head. Disparate times call for disparate measures.

I nod at Beep. "You try."

Her potential usefulness is understandably startling. "Me?"

I provide context. "At this point, I consider you chicken soup, as in, you can't hurt."

A facial twitch nearly turns into a sneer, but she clears her throat.

"Did you do that on purpose... ick?"

Nada.

Dick eyes these goings-on with animal interest. "You expect it to answer?"

"Of course," I say. "We have a certain bond. Confirm this, Beep."

More sodium-free broth than chicken soup, she says, "I guess so?"

Dick's lips purse like the words taste bad. He's thinking about it, wondering if maybe we can ick-chat, and what, if anything, that changes. No slouch in the drugged-brain department, he asks for more specifics.

"I mean, like, can you *hear* it?"

"Absolutely," I announce. "I ask a question, I hear an answer in my head."

When this fails to impress, I again seek the meager corroboration available. "Beep, confirm, this time with gusto, please."

She stares like I'm crazy, but then rinses and repeats.

In a flash, he's the grinning kid who not only figured out the magician's hat has a secret bottom, now he can't wait to ruin it for everyone else. He laughs so hard he repeats the first word of the sentence several times before his engine gets going.

"You... you... you.... You almost had me going, but I'm stoned, not stupid. If it's only answering in your head, how do you know you're not jerking yourself off? How do you know you're not talking to, like, an alien coke dispenser?"

Roused by the rare affirmation, Beep decides to speak. "That's what *I* said!"

My clever plan to remain at ick's side, if, indeed ick *has* a side, upended, I eye-roll so very long and hard, I fear I'll be left sightless. "Beep, never tell anyone outside the family what you're thinking again. In fact, never tell anyone what you're thinking. Especially me."

"Shelley..." she begins.

Revealing my name to the drug-lord-of-the-flies should bother me, but they already have hers from the debit card. Why should she be better known than I?

"Shelley? She your lover?" An amused Dick seems to think he's gotten a step ahead in the chess game. He rubs his chin, attempting to massage his thoughts of us into their proper place.

Hoping to retain some semblance of agency, I say, "Something like that."

Beep ruins it. "Nothing like that."

"She depletes me," I say.

Dick scratches the back of his neck. He pushes a thumb into his cheek. Man, does this guy like touching himself around the face, or what?

A smirkety-smirk. "How'd I miss it? You're crazy, high on that stuff."

"Show's what you know," I say. "It doesn't affect me."

To prove it, I hold up a defiant goo-filled hand and rub it on my upper lip.

His lack of caring infuriates me. "Don't you dismiss me! You're the one putting Descartes before the horse. How do I know I'm talking to ick? How do any of us know anything? How do we know Handy-girl's got bullets in that gun? Beep, repeat!"

"No!"

"Beep, REPEAT!"

When she does, HG unloads a round into the roof, letting in a dollop of light.

This time, I think Beep did crap her pants, because there's this... smell.

"Okay, scratch that. But it really doesn't affect me! I'm special! Tell them, Beep!"

She too busy blushing to back me up, the red on her cheeks almost as bright as the bruised-blue on her nose. I guess she did crap her pants.

Then, sun coming up like a big, bald head, it dawns on me.

It doesn't affect me, but it does affect them.

I look at the goo, then at the backs of their heads.

Beep blinks. She smells something going on, other than what's in her pants, but isn't quite sure what it is. Then it hits her.

"No! Don't! You can't."

Handy-girl turns, unwittingly making herself a better target. "What're you..."

"Can't I?"

"Even if you can, please don't. Shelley!"

A nice big glob splats on Handy-Girl's face. Bald Dick's head is a simpler shot, but I nail it, a second snot-blotch hitting right where he likes to scratch.

Anger rises on their faces, only to subside into the goofiest of smiles. They giggle and point as if seeing each other for the first time. The van veers side to side, but they don't mind that nearly as much as having on those confining pants.

As Handy-girl fights to peel off her too-tight torn jeans, I lean toward the sliding door.

"Come on, open it!" I say to Beep. "It smells like shit in here."

"Sorry," Beep says.

She is sorry. I know she is, because she does as she's told.

And when she does, we jump.

# 8

Leaping from a moving van doesn't hurt quite as much as hitting a tree while rolling downhill, but I'm not fond of either. Friction brings a scratchy halt to my tumbling body's journey. My blurry view settles on the van as it lackadaisically weaves into the distance of this two-bit, two lane street.

We will meet again, Dick and I—once he's done crashing and yanking his pants off.

Meanwhile, there's still the clear and present danger of an unassuming motorist flattening my sweet behind. With ick as ersatz pom-poms, I perform a bizarro-world version of a cheerleader's floor moves, kneeing my way to the shoulder.

Speaking of pants, a wafting aroma tells me Beep and her lower wardrobe have made it as well. I turn away, mostly to protect my nose, and notice an off-brand gas station.

Its cracked plastic sign reads, quite accurately, "Convenience."

"Bathroom, ho," say I.

The walk is quiet. I assume Beep follows but refuse to look back until reaching a chippy-brick wall with facility doors. Yes, she's still with me, a few sheepish paces back. Fortunately (for us, anyway), the Lady's lock is bent to the point of uselessness. The smell inside isn't all that different from Beep, but there's a sort-of working sink, so I leave her to it.

Beyond the sound of running water, paper towels rubbing skin and cloth, and the repeated rush of an air dryer, there's not much going on, so my attention returns to a certain extraterrestrial and its Cinnabon-plus extrusion.

Could it be a defense mechanism, intended to ward off (and entertain) predators? If so, maybe I'm not affected because I'm not perceived as a threat. The way ick's *always* oozing, though, means that despite my calming influence, ick is always stressed. As for why the cream vanishing, I could just ask, so, I do, out loud:

"What happened to all that goo at the police station, ick?"

I get a great big, "Nothing."

This is a problem in more ways than one. Language involving all sorts of neural triggers, leaving me uncertain if I'm getting the *word* "nothing" as in: *Nothing happened to the goo...*

*Or* if ick is the EBE equivalent of an angst-ridden teen responding to a parent. As in: *What're you doing? Nothing. Where are you going? Out.*

*Or* if "nothing" is my way of telling myself ick is being stubbornly silent...

The conjecture conjures Dick's rude observation that I could still be jerking myself off, dazzled to orgasm by my own beliefs. Pleasant as that sounds, I don't accept it. I am not sticking my own words in ick's whatever. There must be more than air between us.

"How can I help you to help me if you won't help yourself?"

"Leave me the fuck alone," comes through pretty clear.

Hearing anything would be a relief, if I didn't also get an image along with the words; my mother leaning against my locked bedroom door as I provide the same reply. It's so vivid, so downright eidetic, it raises questions more than providing answers.

Is ick using my remembrance of things past to communicate, or am I using them on myself? Damn.

One day, when I'm old, I'll look fondly back on my younger self and say, "We are not so different, you and I." And my younger self will answer: "Why the fuck not? I'd hoped to become so much more."

Beep speaks, voice muffled by the door. "Maybe ick has to be near the goo for it to last? Or at least have air contact? That would explain the goo disappearing once the jar was sealed."

She's either eavesdropping or doing a great job at second-guessing. Either way, she having been through a lot, I humor her. "Maybe. You almost done in there?"

Slow and shoulders slumped, she emerges, a bit wet in odd places, but rank no more.

"No more debit cards?" I chide.

"No more."

Rather than repeat the error of trusting her to know things, I add, "Or cell phones."

She pats herself all over and whines. "I don't have it. I must have dropped it."

"Just as well. Where are we in terms of cash on hand?"

She withdraws some soggy bills and peels them apart to count. "Forty-two dollars."

"Change?"

She shoves her hand deep into a wet pocket. It's hard going, but she nods. "Some."

"Beep, oh my Beep, how shall I spend your money?"

The lack of irritation, or, for that matter, affect, tells me she's not feeling herself. Having stopped, we are now in need of rest.

This *the land of a thousand picnic tables*, I spot one on a grassy knoll, comfortably blocked from street-view by Convenience— the gas station, not the word. You see the difficulties language entails? The table is such a sight for sore eyes, if it came with a basket, I'd gladly put all my eggs in it.

"Follow," I say, but not harshly.

The table, of recycled plastic rather than splintery wood, is clean enough to set ick atop. Despite some goo drip-dripping between the slats, ick seems more full-bodied since hitting the windshield, as if somehow replenishing its stores.

Beep slumps onto one bench-seat, I, the other. For a time, we watch the shadows grow long. At least those of us with eyes. In the blessed silence, I ask myself the important questions.

For instance: Who is Kookaburra? What is he laughing about? Is he gay in the old or the new sense of the word? Importantly, why is *he* king of the old bush tree?

Despotism of any sort cannot be allowed to stand. I promise you, Kookaburra, democracy will come one day, and when you're bound with the rest of the tyrants, waiting for your turn to burn, I'll be there to step as close as the air and say to your feathered kingfisher face:

"Not so funny now, is it?"

What do you say to that, eh, Kookaburra?

"Eagle River."

Whoa. I wasn't expecting an answer, let alone a non-sequitur.

Assuming it wasn't Kookaburra, I look to ick. "Was that you, you devil, you?"

Beep's wan expression vaguely asks, "Wha?"

"Not you. Voice in my head. Unbidden."

"Oh?" The exasperation indicates she's feeling better, or at least less numb. I'm about to test that by saying something nasty, when it happens again:

"Eagle River, Wisconsin."

Taking notice, I sit up.

Noticing me, Beep also sits up. "What exactly are you hearing?"

"Eagle River, Wisconsin," I say.

"Eagle what? Bullshit. You're making that up."

Ah, she *is* feeling better. "Think, my dear, think. Why the hell would I make up Eagle River, Wisconsin? I don't even know if it exists."

It is a valid point.

Unexpectedly, so is her response: "Because you're you."

Sigh. It's true. I am me, usually.

I put an arm around the gelatinous pile. "I'm going to need more."

Astoundingly, the bony bits rise and I hear again with my little inner ear:

"Eagle River, Wisconsin."

The slurpy second over, ick, like Citizen Kane saying *Rosebud*, collapses back into a picnic table pool.

Beep is impressed. "Did it… say it again?"

"Yep. Eagle River, Wisconsin. Alien holiday spot, perhaps?" I poke the goo. "Is that where you want to go?" I prod a bony bit. "Do you have people there?"

Nothing. This time, *nothing* in the sense of nothing happening.

I stand and pace. "No, no, no."

Seeing Convenience, I grow once more pleased with the wonder that is me. "I know what we'll spend your money on, Beep. A burner."

She wants to object, thinks she should, but this time curiosity's got a hold on her, so she's off. I wait, in case any additional ick-hint rears, but all my questing questions, inner and outer, only encounter a Zen-like void. Either ick's a big tease, or that last telepathic communication, with its geographic specifics, was exhausting.

And, alas, playing charades is out of the question.

Beep bops back, already googling. "Eagle River's real all right, but dishwater dull. 1400 people and some lakes."

"Context is everything. Try adding UFO."

Beep fingers the phone, then blinks. "Pancakes."

"No, Beep, not breakfast spots, UFO."

She holds up the phone. "I did. I get a lot of entries for Pancake UFO."

What do you know? As it turns out, there's a story there.

I wrote a story once, in middle school, a zombie tale about a guy eking out a post-ap existence. With his days so full of fighting for survival, he no longer sees the z's as individual corpses. They become one big mess of smelly grey with many limbs and rasping heads, a pointless blob he has to hack at or shoot through to get from one brief haven to another.

Having lost everything that made him feel human, he figures he's as pointless as the dead. Rather than accept it, in what quiet moments there are, he prays, meditates, studies whatever great art and literature he can find in the wreckage, ultimately spending more than a decade trying to reclaim the part of himself he considered sacred.

Until one day, climbing hulking ruins as unremarkable as any other, he sees, in a valley below, the biggest freaking horde of dead ever. Only this time, he doesn't see them as a fecund blob. Despite the numbers, he sees the shapes and shadows of the individuals they once were—the men, women, children, who are all still somehow unique, even in death. I go on for pages, describing those corpses, imagining their lives and persona—took me months.

Anyway, at the end of the story, he realizes he's won. He's human again.

That's when they get him.

It's when they got me, too. After reading this page-turner in class I was medicated for the first time. My fictive darkness, coupled with an agitated awareness, and yes, perhaps some other behavior incidents, was taken as a sign of suicidal ideations, schizophrenia, ADD, etc.

"She's too young to know this much of the world's sadness! She must be possessed!"

I maintain that the world, not me, is the problem here, but why split cares? You can't medicate the world. All you can do is hope it doesn't kill itself or go off on a homicidal rampage.

A peal of picnic thunder makes me feel as though something's listening.

Then, of course, like everything else, it fades.

Here, there's another story, gleaned from the Internet by two gals on the lam with a puddle that may or may not be wise. This story is true, but only in the sense that it originated from somewhere other than my head.

On April 18, 1961, in, drumroll please, Eagle River, Wisconsin (!), a flying object, brighter than chrome and resembling "two washbowls face to face with a depressed ring around the middle" landed in the backyard of chicken farmer Joe Simonton. Joe's late morning breakfast interrupted, he headed out to investigate, whereupon the hatch opened, revealing a dark interior. Its substance resembling wrought iron, he later opined it'd make a pretty cool design for a bathroom.

The three five-foot, clean-shaven humanoids that emerged reminded Joe of Italians. Their blue/black jumpsuits did not. When one handed him a large container, Joe *somehow* figured out (and we know how *that* goes) that they wanted water. After complying, he noticed one back inside the ship, doing some cooking on a "flameless" apparatus.

Having been caught mid-brekkie, a still-hungry Joe motioned for a taste. He was presented with four flat cakes, greasy and hot. Game, and apparently not very discriminating, he took a bite. It tasted like cardboard.

Reports claim Joe had the "presence of mind" to preserve the cakes for further analysis. I, however, suspect this was his way of avoiding any insult to the cook.

As in: *Hey, paisan, I'd love to gobble up these yummy puppies, but I gotta, you know, preserve them for analysis.*

Whether Joe called them "pancakes" or that characterization began with researchers remains in doubt. He might've said, "hot cakes" or "lousy cardboard crap."

But rose is a rose is a rose.

Thing is, they *were* analyzed by the Air Force Technical Intelligence Center, whatever the fuck that is, other than, I mean, "technically" intelligent. Upon deformulation (a word contracted from Dick which I use now with some delight) they were found to be composed of flour, sugar and grease. Rumor has it, though, that the wheat in the flour was of an "unknown" variety. Cue X-Files theme.

Much attention ensued, perhaps due to the lack of decent breakfast spots. Soon enough, Joe was complaining that all the (*goldarn*) reporters and their (*damn fool*) questions were keeping him from his chickens.

He went so far as to say, "If it happened again, I don't think I'd tell anyone about it."

He does not, however, mention what he'd say to the aliens should they return. Would he choose honesty, or again simply take the cakes? (*Another analysis? For you, Joe? No problem! I'll just whip up an extra stack here and now!*)

Despite the tale's Paul Bunion tallness, the official explanation *isn't* that Joe was bonkers and/or lying his ass off. Rather, he had a waking dream—his sleeping brain mixing in some kibbles and bits of reality.

Which brings us circle round, to me. Am I, like Ol' Joe, being as honest as I can possibly be about what I ick-hear, but still somehow not telling the truth? Could this Dadaist IHOP story be ick's way of saying we're *not* connected, that language between us is impossible?

No, silly. You can't *tell* someone language is impossible without using language.

But the google now is over, the smartphone and the kings depart. With whatever's chasing us doubtless gaining, I must decide upon consensus reality and proceed accordingly.

"It couldn't be clearer, Beep. We must bring ick to Eagle River, Wisconsin."

# 9

The source of all music is the heartbeat, the source of all story, conflict. Since you can't want what you've already got, that makes any desire a conflict. If I'm here and want to be across the street, or, say, in Eagle River—that's a conflict. Thus, as I sit with Beep at our basketless picnic table, gazing at the grand other of ick, we face the admittedly boring conflict:

"How do we get there from here?"

She attempts to splutter some rational objections but swallows them whole and hits the phone. "It's 286 miles. Amtrak to Milwaukee, three buses, total cost $128, travel time over ten hours. I'm not going to be back home before my folks, am I?"

Surprised she remembers that promise, I reassure her, but only for the sake of order. "Now, now. Catch the lights and you could be back by morning."

"Just me?"

"Indeed. I will be elsewhere. Ick has agreed to take me to its home planet."

Ick shakes like a big bowl full of jelly, reminding me, "That wasn't the deal."

I pat the bunny-blob and smile as if it told a joke. This only makes Beep's incredulity more adamant. She looks at me like I must be mad for not realizing it's all been a game of make-believe.

I opt for partial disclosure: "If you must know, while you were off debit carding us to near-death, words were exchanged. Well… maybe not *words*, but thoughts, certainly. And they were deep thoughts. More than knee-deep, mind you, more than pool-end deep, I'm talking poetry, rife with meaning and portent."

Lips adorably parted, she says, "Were they, now?"

"Please, Lucy. Put a *The Doctor Is IN* sign out and I'll give you a nickel. Do you doubt me?"

"Always."

"Well, don't." Though I hate the gestures, I clear my throat, straighten my clothes and spin about, before feeling calm enough to proceed. "Okay, maybe I wasn't exactly promised a physical journey, but I *was* promised secret knowledge, knowledge which I can only imagine will leave me forever changed and hence on a different path from yours."

Ick farts, as if adding, "You wish."

I scry my savior in a manner intended to remind ick of its vulnerable position. "I'm also thinking we'll need some sort of uncomfortable container in which to carry ick. Perhaps a hermetically sealed plastic bag?"

Ick grows silent.

Beep, surrender-sighing, holds up her remaining buckaroos. "A cheap backpack would wipe us out, and we're already way short for the tickets."

"Even if I go alone?"

"What makes you think... Fine. Yes, even if you go alone."

"So? We'll *steal* the difference."

Some version of an ethical code still in effect, she rears. "You mean, steal money? Forget it. Shoplifting's one thing, but...."

Backing off, I pretend she misinterpreted. "Faith, Beep, faith. I'm not sure what I mean. It's a long way to the bus. On a day such as this, something will present itself, but unless we get started, we'll never learn what it is."

Thus, an epic voyage begins with dull steps on a dull route, me carrying you-know-what, Beep refusing to take turns. After a quarter mile, the boredom begs entertainment, my idle hands grow Mephistophelean.

I shoulder-nudge my naïve companion. "Come on, try the goo! All the cool kids are doing it. Aren't you curious to see if you're immune, too?"

She puts a few quick steps between us. "No."

I have many names—Ol' Nick, Scratch, Beelzebub, Jimmy Jay, Ray. I come closer, swaying my hips seductively, the glistening goo in my arms doing likewise.

"Aw! Why not? Just a dollop? What can a dollop do?"

She picks up speed. "Get away!"

I accelerate. "I will, but only *if* you explain."

"Because not only do I *not* think I'm immune, given how you've been acting, I'm not all that sure you are, either, and if you are it's probably because you're..."

Assuming she's trying to find more interesting words with which to say *fucking crazy*, she fails.

"...fucking crazy! And I already know *I'm* crazy, because I followed you this far, so I don't need to find out."

As agreed, I back off. Seeing as how she's retained her soul, I am a poor excuse for Lucifer. Inwardly, though, I rub my hands and chuckle. *There will be other chances.*

Besides, as the Joel pop goes, she may be right, I may be crazy. It could be me *and* the world. It does get a little dodgy up here sometimes, especially since I ran into ick. Right now, for instance, my head is itchy and I want to cut my hair off, all of it. Only, I want someone else to do it—and I want the other person who cuts my hair off to be me.

Another hundred yawning yards and we near a wide turn. There's a warning-falling-rocks-wall on our left, a steep drop-off to the right, and all around, much sky looking down on the nothing new.

The number of single steps it takes to start this longest journey wore thin at the get-go. I'm sick of it, fed up and gullet-full with this, that and the other, with here, there and everywhere. I'm ready to toss it, pitch a fit, plop ick down the nearest drain and turn my brain over to utter chaos for a refund.

But, wouldn't you know it?

The answer to all our problems (mine, anyway) appears around the bend.

You'd think I'd be thrilled. *I* thought I'd be thrilled, but I find it disappointing. I mean, what does a deus ex mocha latte say about the cosmos? If help arrives just by whining, by virtue of evolution, our groaning planet would swell with cursing, kicking whiners.

Thus, my open letter to the world: MAKE SENSE—damn you!

Then, maybe, I can, too.

Oh, the magic solution? Dick's vanilla van. I know it's his because a) it's the right color and b) it's rammed against a guard rail that kept it from plummeting several hundred yards into some version of wilderness.

Concealing my cosmic disaffection, I smile sweetly at Beep. "See, pouty-pants? I told you a solution would present itself! We've got ourselves some wheels!"

It is indeed the best of all possible turds.

Like Dorothy skipping toward the Emerald City, I prance toward the vehicle.

Beep goes into one of her ten prerecorded phrases. "What do you think you're....?"

I barely reach the driver side when Dick half-tumbles out. He's all smiles and mumbling sighs, not to mention oh-my pants-less. Judging by the keys in hand, turning off the engine was his last sober act.

I answer the question I imagine Beep asked. "Getting us a car. You know Dick was gonna hunt us down, don't you? Now he'll have one less van to do it with. Want to ditch the shocked stare and lend a hand?"

Remembering the gun and poop that went off, Beep shakes her head.

"Can't have that. Think of it as GTA with less compelling characters."

As if defending his persona, Dick's meaty right arm flops over his face, muffling his faint gibbering. It also it shifts the balance enough for his bod to slip further from the seat. Not all at once, oh no. It slow-slides in a sluggish, yet fascinating way, until the fleshy crown of the boy-king's head hits the street with a thud. Following fast, the rest of his body folds backwards in a weird yogic arc, raising his butt and lowering his splayed legs until his toes touch ground.

Interesting as his genitals might be to some, I find myself drawn to the big abrasion on his head. "Ow. That bruise is gonna hurt in the morning, and it's on you, Beep."

"Me? How?"

"Post hoc ergo propter hoc. If you'd acted when I'd asked,

he'd owe you now. Could've come in useful when negotiating for your life. Kinda like taking the thorn out of the lion's paw so you can one day ask not to be eaten."

My beleaguered droog looks ready to soil herself again. "Kidding, Beep! Kidding! You know, I kid, right? All is right with the world."

She humphs back. "Easy for you to say."

"Is it? I think not. I'm in danger, too, physically *and* spiritually. Honestly, I do declare that if I weren't carrying a highly evolved intelligence, my hands would go straight to my hips. What do you say to that, missy?"

"I say... never mind."

Once upon a time, I thought she might actually have some insight into my character, if only by dint of knowing me so long. Over time, her incessant waves of *nevermind* reduced the boulders of my interest to sand, and now act only as a melancholic reminder of why I yearn to part ways.

She grabs Dick's feet to prone his body, finds his frayed jeans and lays them across his face, where he'll be sure to find them when he wakes. I indicate the passenger door.

"Half done is half undone."

Unlike floppy Dick, the semi-conscious Handy-girl doesn't fall. She's slumped forward, forehead to the glove compartment, her back stretched out, exposing pale midriff skin, a *Kilroy Was Here* tramp stamp, and the thing Beep fears most, meaning, the gun—the one Chekov would've insisted go off in the second act. No longer tucked into the rear of her pants, since those have been abandoned, it's somehow balanced behind the thin elastic band of her panties.

I can't help but broach the plot-point. "Should we take it?"

For Beep it's more than a mere weapon; it's a source of trauma, a trigger, if you will—pun intended. As a friend, or at least an echo thereof, I nudge her forward.

"Go on. Face your fear. Touch it. You already touched Dick, how hard can this be?"

Again, pun intended.

As is often the case, she does as she's told, but this time a rare determination takes her features. It's a sort of triumph for her thumb and forefinger to snag the grip and lift. At the same time, behind those two digits remains far more caution than the whole five she used to wipe her ass.

I'm hoping her fear might become fascination, providing us with a useful new toy—until the big party-poop, pun yet again intended, chucks it over the guard rail. A twirling, one-winged blackbird of dark stainless steel, it tumbles out of sight. Pity.

Time a-wasting, Handy is removed, keys procured, and we beam aboard. Beep takes the wheel, I lay ick in the back. The tank nearly full, our phone smarter than I'd hoped, Eagle River is fingered into one Wayz or another, and we're off. In fact, I notice an increased willingness on Beep's to consider the speed limit more a suggestion than an actual law.

I don't ask, but she offers. "If I *can* get back home before my parents, I can say the car was stolen."

"And you'll leave me behind, guilt-free?"

"Nothing's guilt-free with you," she says. "But, that's what you want?"

I cross my heart. "I started this gig nostalgic for a place I've never been, and remain eager-beaver to abandon the lonely place I call home."

Once we're on the Interstate, Blear becomes a rearview speck in both heart and objects-may-be-closer mirror. Then again, it was always a speck, and, as a consequence, always making me feel speck-like.

And yet, and yet, now that I feel speck no more, I'm not sure how to feel.

Now and then, ick gurgles, but I receive no further intrusive ideations.

Or maybe I do, but I'm too tired to notice.

Don't get me started on that again, please.

To return to the dull conflict of distance, Emerson said it's not the destination, it's the journey. Ha. Like it's not the bullet, it's the hole. Wherever Waldo was when birthed that gem, it wasn't here. We pass things. They pass us. Hills, plains, rest stop stores and shopping malls.

If Ralph could find meaning in this stuff, he could find it anywhere.

Ergo, he may as well have stayed home and saved on gas.

To force the time to pass, Beep and I talk in the old way, remembering how, when we were young, we'd never want our parents to leave us alone, but now it's all we seek. Despite some flickering embers of poignant thought, and shared dream, our chat is like a stage play performed once too often, full of feigning, lacking passion or belief.

As we pass a tollbooth scanner, I wonder if Dick will be auto-billed, and thus track us when he wakes. *It*, the pronoun that defines the world, gets dark. The cars behind us do the same. Only their headlights are visible, twinned glowing orbs that float about ominously, pricking my paranoia. We pass urban landscapes of street creeps and crumb creatures, but the land they occupy is so condensed, it does not last long at all.

Passing into Wisconsin provides a liberating rush. I decide my fear of being found may have been misplaced. It's possible that no sense of order whatsoever is involved with me, providing neither passes, nor presenting obstacles. Unlike those who cling to intelligent design, I take comfort in the idea that reality doesn't care about my day, that it is simply moving as it does.

By dawn, the grey dilapidated buildings appearing in the mixed hardwood and coniferous forests, bring more excitement. Why? Because it is here that fiction breeds with fact.

You see, there's this ancient black and white TV interview with Joe Simonton on YouTube. In it, his farm and house are visible in the background. Kissing cousins to Jed Clampett's Ozark's shack, made from wood that long ago lost any color, they're just like the sad structures we see now. Though van windows separate us, I begin to believe we could stop, get out and touch them. At least until the cops are called on us for trespassing.

But we've been there before.

We hit the exit and travel slower roads. Despite some new construction, the YouTube-to-truth ratio grows closer to an equation. We're almost there.

Sensing it, ick borbles like a toddler dreaming of their first taste of ice cream. For the first time since, perhaps, my own screaming birth, I feel forgiving toward the world. Silly ol' world.

I should know better. If reality has a single hunger, it is to prove me wrong.

Beyond the Eagle River welcome sign, despite the cheery, *Great Times Come with the Territory*—an army waits.

Speaking of territory, it looks bigger than the town.

# 10

Power is an illusion.

   Lack of power is an illusion.

Surprisingly, illusions are also an illusion.

Yoko and me? *That's* reality.

Does our van take resplendently to the air, soaring over the tanks and troops as the theme from ET swells in 7.1 Dolby? No, it does not. Beep slams on the brakes. Ick wobbles with the suspension.

Not a good move. The eagle-screech of balding tires is likely to draw attention, and I doubt we'd survive a traffic stop. Too late to correct her now. I can only hope there will be time for recriminations later.

"Now what?" Beep asks.

"You couldn't ask that *before* hitting the brakes?"

Ah, so there *was* time for recriminations. Excellent.

As to what comes next, there's a reassuring lack of movement from the army down the road, providing a sense of salvation a la mode. That doesn't mean it will stay that way.

Immediate question: Once they spot us, will all that hardware blow us straight to heaven, and/or, simply, *up*? If so, peeling out, pedal to the metal, would add but a few more moments to our final day. Assuming they want ick, though, I'm guessing they won't hurt us, but who wants to guess about that shit? This is why there are no atheists in foxholes, or perhaps only atheists.

Oh, and the dead.

It's *possible* their presence is a coincidence, that these tanks and troops have gathered to honor a local vet's centennial birthday. *Or...* maybe they're not here for ick, but they're after the same thing ick is, the ride home. Could be something hovers in the Eagle River sky, unseen by the naked eye (as opposed to an eye dressed to the nines), making pancakes as it awaits ick's arrival.

"How's this, Beep? Back up slowly, see if they advance."

She does. They don't.

After a few yards, I slap her. "For fuck's sake, don't *keep* driving backwards! The idea is not to stand out. Make a youey— nice and slow, see?"

I get a rapid nodding. The three-point turn takes four, an automatic road-test failure, but given the narrow road, it wouldn't single us out as attempting to flee with an extra-terrestrial.

As away in the opposite direction, there is an unexpected wrinkle, which, of course, I should have expected; ick pulses and bloops like clear tapioca coming to a boil.

In my head, it says, loudly: "Eagle River, Wisconsin!"

On the one hand, I am more convinced than ever it is ick with which I speak. On the other... "No way, bubbles. Even I'm not ballistic enough to head straight into a platoon."

Prissy ick goes all gurgling. "Eagle River, Wisconsin!"

"No!"

"Eagle River, Wisconsin!"

"No!"

"Eagle River, Wisconsin!"

"No!"

Beep stares at me, then ick. "You *are* talking to it!"

I get screechy. "Yes, I'm talking to it! What proof do you require? Want to see me do it while drinking a glass of water?

"Okay! I believe you!"

Now that she does, I'm not sure I do. I mean, ick could still be some alien Alexa with language recognition and a proximity alarm."

"What's it saying?"

Ick seems to understand Beep-words, too, because I hear it yet again, louder, if that's a thing: "Eagle River, Wisconsin!"

I translate. "The alien equivalent of *are we there yet?*"

She slows but doesn't stop. "What do you want to do?"

I surrender to my survival instinct with a scowl. "Turn around and head home. Given the tanks, a life of quiet desperation suddenly doesn't seem so bad."

"Eagle River, Wisconsin!"

I grit my teeth and howl. "But first maybe we should leave our semisolid friend here at a yard sale with a little note stuck in it, saying *Free!*"

Then ick says something new: "Remember our deal!"

Over the whirr of the engine, I hear my heart thumping. My eyes narrow.

"It *is* a deal, then, is it?"

"Yes."

Beep staring, the stakes rising, I decide to be uncharacteristically fair and deal her in. "Stop talking in my head, ick. It's crowded enough as it is. Bubble so she can see. Once for no, twice for yes. Got it?"

A bubble rises and pops. Another follows, making two.

"Oh my god," Beep says. "I wish I had a camera. This is... historic."

Admitting, with a humble sigh, my significance, I cooperate. "Check the burner."

"Oh yeah, right." Beep checks our toy. "It does. It's got a camera."

We drive until comfortably out of sight of the 4077th and stop on the shoulder.

Recalling the last time I didn't state what I thought obvious, I decide not to take chances. "No posting on social media, okay?"

"I'm not an idiot."

"Let me hear you say it."

"No posting on social media." She raises the phone to the popping pool. "All set."

"Okay, ick, time for the big questions," I say. "You and I have a deal, right?"

Two bubbles.

"My end is to get you where you're going, somewhere in Eagle River, Wisconsin, right?"

Two big bubbles.

"In exchange, you reveal your transcendental alien knowledge, the meaning of human life, more specifically, what *I* am in the scope of things."

Beep lowers the phone. "You want a blob to tell you what you are? *I* could tell you that, Shelley. You're a God-damned, fucking..."

I pick the best of all possible words. "Lunatic, yes, I know. It's answers like that, heard all my life, that make me yearn for something deeper. Now hush your sad little human mind, so we may better attend ick's responsive farts."

Her lips curl into a snarl, but she looks back at the phone.

"Ick, you get to where you need to be, I get to know myself, yes?"

The first bubble rises slowly, the second follows fast.

"That was yes, right, Beep?"

She nods. "Yes, it was a clear yes."

I should relish her agreement, but, as usual, it gives me pause. I've been so distracted by the question of whether we're actually communicating, a more insidious possibility hadn't occurred to me.

Beep lets loose with an unkind impersonation of yours truly. *"You wouldn't lie to me, would you?* Seriously, you may as well ask how often it beats its children."

"First, I don't sound anything like that. Second, so what? If naivety is all you have to proceed with, does that mean you should never proceed?"

She shrugs in a shruggy way, expressing the whole of her shruggy being. "Yes! Maybe that's *exactly* what it means."

I put a finger to her forehead and tap at her heart's bony home. "What you're feeling in there? That's the difference between us. And while yes, there is medication for that, I've neither the strength, nor the interest in becoming less me, and more you."

Her head wobbles, bobble-like. "But you *are* willing to try to sneak past an army?"

"As Lyndon Johnson said at the White House barbeque, these are the steaks.

Head still a-wobbling, the elusive creature known as Beep

scans her surroundings, searching for hidey-holes and escape routes.

"We don't even know where to take it, exactly."

"Ah, but we do. A reliable narrator? Maybe not. Mr. Bubbles could be a big fat liar. A reliable compass, though? Yeah, baby." I aim a thumb at the puddle. "The ick-kettle's been on the boil since we got here, more as we approach, less when we retreated. All we have to do is dare follow."

All thumbs, Beep juts hers back toward town so hard, it's like she's throwing her hand away. "How do we get past all that?"

I think. True, I always think, but this time, I come up with a cunning and brilliant plan, one-part gumption, two-parts ick.

"The van has served its purpose. From here, all we need is a bucket and a dream."

Ick head-screams, "No! No hermetically-sealed bucket!"

My, my. Either our connection is growing in logic leaps and emotional bonds, or the little bastard's been listening a lot more than it lets on. I explain that said bucket wouldn't be at all like the plastic bag threatened back in Blear., but it does little to calm the miniature roiling sea.

It's only when Beep says, "We have to find something to hide you in," does blobby shut it down. The implication that she has some pull is another surprise. No doubt ick was simply taken aback that Beep, without Barbie-like pretense, was speaking to it as if they were both living beings.

We find a Home Depot. Beep holding the cash, me wanting to be sure we get the most bucket for her money, we debate leaving ick behind. I see little risk of passerby peering in and mistaking ick for an infant or pet left in a hot car. Vomit, maybe, but nothing worth moral outrage. After some haranguing, Beep agrees, and ick doesn't get a vote. As we make for the box store, though, part of me feels like I should have left a chew-toy.

Inside, we quickly settle on the ten-gallon rope-handle job, because it is on sale. An otherwise fulsome cashier grimaces at our crumpled oh-so-tender legal tender but is mollified by Beep's muttering efforts to flatten the bills.

Without further incident, we return to the van. Which is to

say, sure, there are incidents, but only if you'd care to elevate some aisle gazing and meandering among irrelevant shoppers to such a haughty status. At this stage, despite whatever ambience it may provide, I will not indulge such incidentals. Suffice it to say, none of it is nearly as interesting as, say, a rubber ball lying in the mud, or a red wheelbarrow beside white chickens.

We curve round to box-store back, where blacktop lot meets fallow field, ditching the Dick-van far from the Madding Marines. There, with the fussy loveless love of an impatient mom dressing a toddler, I scoop ick into its new home.

I want to say ick likes it, but all that churning could mean anything from an allergic reaction to joy to suffocation. I could ask, but such a query would only raise false hope. It's not as if we're about to get back in line to exchange one rub-a-dub-tub for another that could be equally rough on baby's sensitive skin.

I smile warmly at the clear pudding. "Deal with it."

Less warmly, I turn to Beep. "Go on, pick it up, already."

If I'm playing mom, she's the distant dad, tiredly wondering how he got himself into all this. Realizing I am not her beautiful wife, nor this her beautiful house, she hefts the handles, avoiding the poo-poo contents at all costs.

Like Jack and Jill up the hill, we enter the field.

Ick produces a brand-new sound. The result of physics, it is not will or meaning full, only a sloshing, in tune with our trudging gait. My earlier compass analogy holds, however. Plod one way, the bubbling slows. Another, it picks up. Regardless of the creature's comfort, the teen witches and their scrying bucket are definitely headed somewhere.

Our need to remain out of sight means no beeline to be had, but our intentional wavering soon delivers an upward scenic view of little town, visiting military, and a snaking river I assume is named Eagle.

The picture postcard distance and lack of an immediate death-threat tempers my initial assessment. Army may have been an exaggeration but, hey, give me a break. It's only in terms of sneaking around and/or through them, that their particulars grow in importance.

To wit: In a little old town all covered in brine, roll twelve little tanks in two straight lines. Barely fitting side-by-side on the main drag, they block the modest traffic. Meanwhile, support vehicles linger on side streets as sundry foot-soldiers, tromping with machinelike purpose, gather in six open lots.

I want to say these are *our* brave lads and lassies, (USA, USA, make Gog and Magog Great Again, etc.), but the lack of insignia makes their loyalty yet another of the many exciting unanswered questions life has to offer. Paramilitary? Paranormal Military? Regardless, the practical designation is *them*. Not giant ants, old monster film fans, but an *us-vs-them* deal. Myself, ick, and, if you must include her, Beep, comprise *us*, they're *them*.

With an efficiency terribly impressive to someone who's only seen local football teams and cheerleaders try to line-up, the troops enter formation. In groups separated by pairs of those support vehicles, they follow the Madeline tanks northeastward, ho.

Repeating the image before us, rather than adding anything new, Beep says, "They're leaving! Where are they going?"

Whatever delight might be had in watching the withdrawal, is drowned by a sad, undeniable knowledge. "Where do you think? Exactly where we plan to go."

"Shelley!"

Rather than congratulating me for my brilliant, penalty-free deduction, she's tilted bucket-ways, looking like she wants to drop it. Within, ick threatens to boil over and make a mess of her nice, clean consciousness. If we had the right china, we'd have a tea-cup tempest.

I approach and put a delicate finger to my pouty lips. "Hold please, ick, while we plot a path. We're nearly as much strangers in this strange land as you."

A bit of waving goo breaches the top. Beep leaps half a foot.

My evil eye defers. "Very well. Set ick down for now."

Once on terra firma, ick seems to calm, Beep does not.

"I nearly touched that gunk!"

"So? Some rise to drug abuse, others have it thrust upon them."

"I'd rather it be neither."

"Must it always be about you, Beep?"

The frail thing near exhaustion, we take a breather, away from our foreign client, closer to the vista. For some idiot reason, I expected to see more of the petrified wood farms spied on the road and in that five-decades old YouTube interview. Instead, no longer famed as hosting Joe Simonton's Interplanetary House of Pancakes, vacation homes with docks dot the river, along with rental shops for ATVs, boats, and fishing gear. The streets contain B&Bs, upscale coffee spots and a children's museum. It is, in short, a touristy, family friendly place.

"Beep, a google and a peck, please. What is Eagle River about these days?"

She complains, but having something to do will cheer her in no time.

"The Eagle River/Three Lakes chain boasts the largest number of inland interconnecting lakes in the world. That's 28 lakes, folks. Count 'em, 28, and hundreds of wilderness trails"

See? She's trying to be funny, like me. Isn't that sweet?

"Trail-map?"

Her try ends in sighs. The cheap, yet shockingly reliable, battery has given up the ghost, cruelly severing our connection to the vast store of virtual knowledge.

"Never mind, then. With all those trails, we can crisscross around whatever, and what we don't know, I can always make up."

"Right."

The one-word response is packed with meaning, but the packaging is so nice, I've not the heart to tear it open.

Ick no longer seething, I chin-point to the bucket. "Come along, Watson, the goo is afoot."

Eyes heavy, she makes a half-assed effort then slumps. "Could I just... maybe... get some coffee before we go fight the tanks? I'm not sure how much longer I can stay awake."

"Coffee?"

"It's stupid."

"It *is*, Beep, it is, yet your words touch my heart. More than that, they make my nostrils flare, as if detecting that delightful, bittersweet aroma hovering among these cooler airborne molecules of moss, leaf, and dirt."

"Sorry I asked."

"Don't be, not without permission."

I weigh what we see of the town. The troops have left, but either they already scared most everyone away, or we've arrived off-season. "Let's do it."

"Are you sure?"

"Oh, for... take yes for an answer, will you? Take it. Take it! Ere I force it down your gullet, thou globby bottle of cheap, stinking chip oil!"

Thus, we make our waddling way to the quiet streets. The locals that remain appear far too bebothered by the memory of tanks to pay much attention to two sweet teens and their tub. That is, until, on a narrow avenue, two touring hipsters appear across from us—carrying the exact same tub as we! They gaze our way awhile, then, with smile and nod, move on.

The surreal and socially awkward encounter leaves us slack-jawed. Have we stumbled into a CE3K Devil's Tower thing, where select humans get a free alien-in-a-bucket, as long as supplies last? After many fluttering blinks, I figure it out.

"The tub was on sale. Lots of good fishing in these parts. What does that tell you, Beep?"

"They think we're carrying our catch."

"Watson, you've outdone yourself, so, double-indubitably."

"And if someone looks inside?"

"Tell them it's a jellyfish, or we're into collecting sick. Coffee?"

Hailing from a one-Starbucks town, it's curious to see several fresh caffeine providers. We select one that looks both empty and soulless; *Espresso Yourself.* And the smell, dear sweet lord, the exquisite smell, perks us all on its own. The only bad news is that a quick count of remaining funds yields only enough for a single espresso latte.

Unless I can chug it all down while Beep pays, we'll have to share.

The sole occupant is a bereted barista, who, in true fake

beatnik mode, reads a copy of *On the Road*. At first, neither our bucket nor our eye-candy selves earn as much as a glance. Innocuousness may be a plus in terms of our mission, but I still want to harrumph. It's not until Beep waves to indicate our existence that the order is given.

Ground beans are scooped and leveled. Once attached to the hot-to-trot god-body of the blessed machine, black honey drips from portafilter to cup and the frothing wand hiss foams the soy. Lo, the paper chalice is filled, topped and presented complete with sleeve and plastic top.

I feel my tongue-tip burning already, as the unfortunately closer Beep stretches to receive the dark, liquid manna. Such a short distance, and yet, somehow, along that inches-long gap between the barista's hand and Beep's, it all goes horribly, horribly awry.

The precious cup is dropped.

Beep cries, "What the fuck?"

I try to catch the falling drops midair. Not fast enough, I put all that enraged energy into a death-ray glare trained on the barista, expecting either him or his beret, to immediately set to work again, and perhaps offer two cups to make up for the incompetence.

Despite all my rage, I'm a smashed pumpkin rat in cage. The beatnik looks right through me, or rather, over and beyond my stunning wonderfulness, to someone behind us.

Someone in uniform.

Shit. Not *all* the troops have left town. Worse, this crew-cut fellow's got a shotgun shine with a blue moon in his eyes, the lean, hungry look of which Caesar warned. And, oh yeah, a sidearm pointing our way.

On the plus side, Beep does not crap her pants. Maybe a man in uniform engenders more confidence than a drug addict, maybe she's yet to switch emotional gears and is still pissed about the lost latte. Mostly likely, her irritated bowls are empty. We haven't eaten in ages.

Soldier-boy waves for us to move. Not knowing if his gun is locked and loaded, or what that means (something to do with a rifle and John Wayne?) we comply.

As we move, I give him a piece of mind, mine: "If you think I'm going to thank you for your service now, you can just forget it."

Ignored, I try to think of how to blame Beep for this fiasco. Coffee being her idea, I sense a semi-valid argument. But how to neutralize my enthusiastic agreement? I know, I'll say it never happened. Works for politicians, why not me? Here's the church, here's the steeple, open the door, here are the sheeple.

Time disallows it. As our Maynard G. Krebs barista freeze-gawks, Soldier-boy herds us, bucket and all, out the back, into what is probably Eagle River's only alley.

We are not, however, forced into a waiting personnel carrier and whisked to an underground base where we must swallow our distrust for the Military Industrial Complex and join forces to battle an ancient evil. Nor do we meet a gruff, battle-hardened commander who knows an enemy when he sees one and doesn't give a rat's ass what those lab-bound boffins are trying to tell him about trying to communicate with that... that... *thing*.

Nope. None of that.

Instead, kicking the shop door closed behind us, Soldier-boy presents us with the return of an exciting guest star. Unexpected, that is, to all but me—for fate has once again reared its incoherent, babbling head to confirm my original leap of intuition.

It's Dick.

It's always Dick, isn't it?

Forever and ever, it's Dick, Dick, Dick.

# 11

"Hi," Dick says.

"Hi," I say back.

I coyly wave my fingers, not only as mere greeting. It's a tough one-in-a-million shot, but if I conjure my inner superhero, I can save the day, ick-dipping my digits then executing an acrobatic twofer; a graceful booger flick-back at Soldier-boy, followed by a swift Dick double-snot. Having lacked a Black Widow action figure as a child, however, I was denied the proper plastic role model, and so decide against it.

Besides, my old nemesis has learned some new dog tricks.

"Put the pail down slowly, and step away from it, fast. Now."

Soldier-boy kisses the back of Beep's head with the gun.

"Don't want to do that," I warn. "Irritable bowel syndrome. Besides, it's not a pail, it's a tub."

Fortunately, her sphincter holds. Once we're a satisfactory distance from our bucket-buddy, SB lowers his head to scratch his red neck. This is no ethno-political comment; his neck is red from being scratched a lot. I nudge for Beep to take note.

"He's hooked on more than soy mocha lattes. I'm guessing Dick's his personal barista."

Beep finds her voice, right in her throat, where she left it, but seems a bit confused as to who the enemy is here.

"First, you're Jodie Foster, now you're Veronica Mars?"

"A marshmallow? No way. That is so two generations past."

Dick loosens a little and smiles, I assume, at our banter.

"You... you're funny," he says with a wag of finger.

Arms cross. "Indeed, I've heard tell of such legends."

"Aren't you gonna thank me?" he asks.

Eyeing this Wonderful Wizard of Odds, I raise an eyebrow. It's meaning is inherent in the context, but Beep comes out and asks, "Thank you for what?"

"Not having him put a bullet in the back of your head. You'd never know it was coming, until it was too late."

I go into Resting Disapproval Face. "Actually, I'd never know at all, what with being dead, but, okay, I'll bite. Why not kill us, Dick? Is it that you *won't* kill us because we serve some purpose, or that you *can't* kill us, because in terms of archetypes you're… I dunno, either A) a male version of the whore with a heart of gold or B) a scrupulous drug dealer, who does what he must to get by, but has ethical lines he will not cross?"

Beep begins to free-verse mutter, loudly, yet still so guttural, there are no words to be had. When she starts stamping her feet, I suspect the dregs in her intestines have backed up into her brain. It's embarrassing. Not just for her, for me. Riveted by the ants-in-pants-dance, the part of Dick's face around his mouth, just that part, mind you, wrinkles.

"Calm down. I don't go around shooting people, but it doesn't mean I won't if I have to."

I check a mental survey box. "B then."

Still stamping, Beep eyes the alley floor. A thoroughly-lost expression swims along the deep end of Dick's face, "You're crazy. Really crazy."

"There were several diagnoses to that effect," Beep says.

I laugh. "That you know of, Beep, that you know of!"

Dick snaps his finger repeatedly, as if he didn't already have our full attention, "Hey, hey, hey. We're in a situation here, right? For everybody's sake, try to keep it real, okay?"

"If this is real, you can keep it."

"Just listen. You can't do shit to stop me from taking that alien whatsis, but the Area 51 tank squad can, and, I sure as fuck don't want them on my ass the rest of my life. The reason we're talking *at all* is because, I'm thinking, on the off chance you *can* talk to it…"

I interrupt. "Not *it*, ick. Beep and I have been through this already."

"...maybe you could find out why the stuff evaporates, if there's a workaround."

It's such a simple solution, I nearly up-chuckle. "Is *that* all, Dick?"

We're both wondering if Beep will ever chill, when a squeaky-squawk erupts from one of the many pockets in Soldier-boy's uniform.

"Angel 12, report. Where the hell are you?"

I'm no audiophile, but he's getting nice sound from such a small speaker, a little on the trebly-side, sure, but not so much that it doesn't make Soldier-boy's face drop so low he doesn't bother picking it up.

Dick puts a "shh!" finger to his lips, while SB hurriedly presses a finger to himself and says, "Sir, still in town, sir. I was delayed. On my way."

"Negative. Stay put. Got some local chatter about a gun at a coffee shop. Probably BS, but we're sending a team. Rendezvous 1300 at Spruce and Division."

SB's eyes roll way, way, up into his head. "Copy."

I'm not going to tell him the gun they're reporting is *his*, but from the lightning fast way his hand goes to the handle on the *Espresso Yourself* door, I figure he already knows.

My bald nemesis, seeing his source of phallic piercing power about to vanish like morning goo, tries putting the Dick back in dictator. "Don't...!"

But we're way past that. Soldier-boy doesn't bother with so much as a glance at his supplier. "It's not worth it, man."

And there he goes, off and running, late, late, for a very important date. Briefly, I worry he'll shoot the beatnik witness, but the lack of gunfire is a comfort.

Meanwhile, back here in the alley...

"Shit!"

Anger comes off Dick in waves so hot you could fry an egg on him. Me, I lean back against the cool alley wall. It's not cold, it's just totally cool—it looks cooler still with me leaning on it.

"Didn't figure on the barista, eh, Moriarty?"

Gunless, his only move is to try for the bucket. Beep, her dance complete, puts a toe to the edge, like she's ready to kick it at him.

"Impressive, Beep! Did you have some action figure I don't know about?"

He comes to a stumbling stop. "Shit!"

Doing my bit, I wet my fingers and dare him closer. "Come on, Dick, you and me, here and now, let's waltz our way over the Reichenbach Falls!"

"Shit!"

A whirlybird rush intrudes from above. Dick looks both ways, almost at the same time, then runs for the street. The real surprise? Beepety-Beep, without so much as a by-your-leave, follows in his footsteps, leaving me and the bucket behind. Has she lost it?

Exasperated, betrayed, I cry out: "Hey, that cost money!"

Given how fast she moves, it may not be so much a betrayal as a desperate search for a bathroom. I, then, must make do with goo. Eschewing the container, I scoop as much ick as I can into my arms and hoof it after my fleeing friend.

Beep's mid-street when a single copter appears in the northern sky. Thinking it's after us, she screams, cries and runs, attracting what little attention there is. Still, Eagle River is so small, all it takes is a two-block dash to bring us to its outskirts.

An aged shed, worthy companion to Singleton's lost farm, half-hangs in the river. Beep enters, I follow her panting moans. Satisfied there will be no imminent intestinal evacuation, we sit.

Unlike the brick wall, the dirt ground is cool in the sense of temperature. Slats of sunlight swarm from copious gaps between wall-boards, bright and blinding should your head move the wrong way. The sound of chopper-slashing blades, overwhelming the water and the wind, make things seem worse than they are.

Beep embraces a new mantra: "We've got to get out of here, we've got to get out of here."

The delusion is so finely structured, I understand why she's lost in it, but this is exactly the sort of self-fulfilling fear than can *make* things worse than they are.

"Shh. I know it feels like we're in the scene where the criminals are cornered but you've got to breathe and think. *We* don't have a gun. *We're* not drug dealers. It's Soldier-boy and Dick they're after, not us."

"I ran out of the coffee shop with him!" she howls. "They must have seen!"

Purveyors of fictive realities may, from their butt-chairs and couches, judge Beep a wuss, but at the moment, she, panicked and hyperventilating, is being more human than you. While I, as we have seen, am not so much brave, as desolately crazy.

"We don't *know* they saw us. We don't have a shred of evidence, direct or circumstantial, that they know we're here."

"Dick saw us! He knew we were in that coffee shop. If he can follow us, why not them?"

Oh, dear. Good question. My hesitation doesn't help, rather it tightens around her heart and lungs, making the pressure rise. This is bad. If the soldiers hear her jabbering and find us, they'll bring her in for sure, if only for medical treatment and I don't see her keeping secrets under pressure.

If only I had *something* to calm her down, something to force her to relax, to make her smile, to help her let her hair down. Not to mention her pants.

Oh yeah. I do.

A flick of the wrist and two viscous drops strafe Beep's cheek and chin. Touching the spots, rubbing goo between her finger-pads, she horrified, teary-eyed.

"What did you do? What did you do?"

Once the high kicks in, she'll thank me for it. I'm sure.

"Relax. Go with the flow. Dick didn't seem any worse for wear."

I do wonder whatever became of Handy-girl, but decide it best not to mention that now.

Her breathing deepens, but it's still so fast, I feel her heart pounding. The ick is having an effect, but it's not the joyful surrender I expected.

Imaginary notepad in hand, I ask: "What are you feeling, exactly?"

"I'm so comfortable Shelley, but I don't like it. I don't like it. It's dangerous. I don't like feeling so comfortable."

I play along. "No reason why you should."

I wish people thought more often to mirror me. It helps.

"I see you. I see you so much."

She tries to touch my cheek. I let her. "Of course, you do."

Mayhaps panic delayed the high? At least the roaring blades have grown beside the point.

"The light, it keeps slicing you up. And I have to keep putting you together, over and over."

I nod. "Because you're my friend."

She shakes her head. "No. Maybe, sometimes, but this is over and over and over, and I don't want to do it anymore. I don't, but anyway, I do. It's been going on for as long as the sunlight, so long it's not a choice, I have to do it. I can't stop."

Whoa. Is this what people feel like when they talk to me?

I pally-punch her shoulder. "Sure you can, Beep! Take a break. Smoke 'em if you've got 'em. You've earned it. I'll uh… put my slices together myself for a change."

She leans closer to whisper a secret.

For the first time ever, something haunted in Beep's tone makes me afraid. "You don't understand. You think you do but you don't. The elves and fairies and ghosts and aliens, and all the birds in Disneyland? They're begging me to tell you all about it. But they're mechanical, stuck in a loop, and, I don't want to do it for them. I did once, I swear, there was at least one time that I wanted to tell you everything, but now I don't."

"Why?"

Wind whips through the walls, rattling the boards, swallowing my question with sound and fury. The chopper must be lower to the ground. Maybe I hear voices, but, more to the point, if we *are* found, I've only swapped one crazy version of Beep for another.

If she passes out, I can pretend she's drunk.

"Beep, could you lie down and close your eyes?"

"I can't ever close my eyes. Not ever."

Instinctively defiant, she tries to stand, but falls backward, and yes, the pants come off. She still doesn't seem to be enjoying it very much, though.

"Not ever, not ever, not ever."

Oh, how I hate being the most realistic one in the room! But other than a bubbling slime pool, I'm the only other here. "Beep, whatever it is, it doesn't matter. Nothing matters. Just. Calm. Down."

"Not ever, not ever, not ever. I won't! I won't! I won't."

As if my bright idea couldn't backfire any further, she gets up and tries to bolt.

I grab for her, but her naked arm slips from my gooey grip, and she's out. "Beep!"

I plop ick in the dirt and follow.

The helicopter is way too low. Beep runs toward it, arms flailing as if trying to fly herself. I can't hear what she's screaming, but I think it's still: "I won't! I won't!"

I was right about one thing; we weren't in danger before. The chopper doesn't give a fuck about her, or me, not at all. Both pilot and gunner are focused on the only other figure on the street who isn't running.

It's Soldier-boy, gun out and pointed up.

The men in the flying machine don't like that at all and they have bigger guns. A voice booms from yet another mighty fine sound system.

"Drop your weapon or we will open fire!"

There's a lot of major loons about today, and Soldier-boy is one. Maybe the army was all he had, and with that clearly gone, he has nothing left. He fires at the copter, one round after another, as if he can bring it down.

Turns out, he can.

Son of a bitch.

Something sparks along the fuselage, then smokes. The chopper wobbles and drunk turns, like it's decided to bag this crap and mosey on back home. It doesn't make it. As if the very idea a hunk of metal could fly was ridiculous to begin with, it falls.

And Beep is right beneath it, pants-less and flapping her arms, as if the idea of flight isn't ridiculous at all, that it's the best thing ever.

There is fire. There is red and orange. There is black and there is white. And heat—a flush of sunlight, like leaving a dark house midday, only rather than carpe diem, you've shoved your head in an oven set to broil.

Ahead of me there are a score of crunching burning things. They could be metal, branches, twigs, or bones but I realize

Beep must be among them.
  I realize Beep is dead.

# 12

My heart is a bunch of twisting nonsense. I am sundered, left in pieces, broken and disavowed. True, I always was, but now, Beep is dead. I wished her gone, yes, not harmed. To be more precise, I didn't wish *her* gone, I wished *me* gone. She was supposed to stay, so I could love her from afar, far, far, afar, to satisfy my undying ache to claw free of our childhood cage, by tearing out what there was of her inside me, so I could, at last and forever, begin to begin anew.

Might we then have met again?

I wouldn't have held my breath, but, sure, anything's possible.

Without her, though, the cage is all that's left, and I'm the opposite of free. Why? Because each human met creates in us a score of sensations, overt, magnificent, mundane, sublime. Deprived of source, I no longer sense her or her Beepitude, just the neural echoes she left behind. And what good are those? All they do, all they can do, is sit and wait, occasionally reassembled by memory's cookie cutter, in a frail effort to justify some shallow narrative.

Or worse, to justify a whim.

Yet now, to forget what I yearned to, to leave what I longed to, becomes a total eradication, a Beep homicide. Besides, what can be left of my journey if I've no place to leave?

"Eagle River, Wisconsin."

"Fuck you, ick."

I stumble back numbly to the wood-shedded puddle-jumper. Three bubbles appear in rapid succession. A pause, they pop, then repeat, all three. It's as if ick wants to extend our double-bubble language to include a nonbinary *maybe*.

I shake my head. "Not happening. Not in the mood. Not ever. I've given you too many words already."

"We have a deal."

Outside, sirens shriek with magpie enthusiasm. Sooner or later, someone will point at our hidey-hole and say, "That poor dead girl came running out of there!"

And a murder of crows will arrive.

Like a new mourner asked permission to harvest the organs of the deceased, I have to decide. Even if it's deciding not to decide, I must take part. Wasted and core wounded, the death of hope doesn't seem so bad anymore, but I feel obliged to consider the possibility I may someday grow curious about life again.

Then why not suffer one more scene? I already have enough regrets for one day.

Ick projects a particular helplessness. Specks of earth, wood, grass and maybe-bones hang in there like eye-floaters in vitreous humor.

I lift the water-flavored Jell-O that is now my only friend. Together we leave the shack, not through the front door, beyond which things yet burn, but waist-deep riverside. The attention of the Eagle River world-machine riveted on the chaos, I proceed on the down-low along the bank. The water flowing my way, unhindered by anything other than myself, I follow the river north, taking to bush or eddy whenever it's unclear if the coast is clear.

Smoke and crackle, hue and cry, town and trouble left behind, the soothing quality all rivers share is on the rise. I debate a brief dive below, to wash something nameless off me, to rid ick of the flotsam within, but I don't know what effect the water might have on the alien albatross. Given how my Beep experiment turned out, I turn my back on science.

Better to be dirty than dissolved, no?

Ick tight in my lovin' arms, I feel every bit of quivering fizz, making it easier to tell which way to go. Whenever the toil and trouble get to be too much for me to keep my grip, my gel-belly pet kindly recalibrates. Ignorant of town and time, we head up into the woods. This forest is real, unlike Blear's junk-pine dumpers, where things were always falling with no one there to hear, this place is dense with breathing trees and probably home to animals. Among the trails, I sneaky-sneak and think of Beep, wondering why I can't remember anyone else in a remotely pleasant way.

Most of the world I rejected myself, so no surprises there. My parents? They loved me indeed, until, I became indecipherable. After that, they loved just as fiercely, but I was not the recipient. They adored what they thought I was, or what they hoped I'd become, leaving the me of the moment as invisible as the air.

Did I do the same to Beep? No, I had no hopes for her future, and ignoring her was always an active effort.

Am I tired of feeling sorry for myself, yet? Almost. But exhaustion changes nothing. Beyond divine, or extraterrestrial, intervention, I doubt anything could. If nothing else, I am so set in my gilded rut, that were I presented with an exquisitely detailed map leading all the way from the first hominid down to me, a guide that included all the ecstatic triumphs and crushing foibles of humanity, complete with graphs, charts and footnotes, that brought the all and everything completely into the context of me, it *still* couldn't tell me what it is a man is, let alone a woman, let alone a me. How dare it even try?

It's why I put my faith where the sun don't shine, in chaos, that eager, stronger lover that all supposed reality holds back in order to be real, the dark gloppy waters above which the spirit of God hovered prior to separating day from night for their own good.

Trees for the forest. Slices for the after pie. There is no end to world, woods and words, but they cool with darkening, leaving less and less to steer me, save the cradled bubbling which faithfully, selfishly, provides direction.

If only it would mention the obstacles, like rocks. Ow.

Animal crunches of branch and leaf arise from near-shadows. Rather than sway me, they make me smile to think—Beep would've soiled herself by now. The appearance of headlight is another matter, jeeps rolling on paths intended for hiking boots. They tell me, in a language that leaves no doubt, exactly where *not* to head. Despite ick's effervescent protests, I work my way around them, again and again, but their frequency increases.

We must be in their territory, whatever land, for whatever purpose, that the military's cordoned off. This is it, then, a final chance to set it all aside, to give up the ghost, or, in our current genre, the EBE.

The passages of my achy-breaky heart aside, I do still *want* to get to the end, alone or not, mad or sane, innocent or criminal, kind or cruel, smart or foolish, lovely or repulsive, in body and/ or soul. And, *yes*, I hold out hope for a reward at painbow's end, that divine intervention that will magick all things into their place, and me into mine.

A hill backlit by glowy haze makes ick quite randy. I admit to feeling a bit romantic myself. It reminds me of our first hill together, where my unfathomable lover and I met, and where, in an effort to see ick, I tried to get you to see the ball.

It didn't work, of course, but with memories interlinking as they do, another ball comes to mind. Not Cinderella's, no, this was a ball I gave to Beep years ago, as a gift, because she said it looked a bit like the one she'd loved and lost.

I didn't tell her it *was* her ball, or that I'd stolen it, along with several other toys. But I *did* give it back, and, moreover, my sinful omission was not entirely selfish. I prefer credit for my wickedness, but, Beep looked so very happy thinking me her savior, I couldn't bring myself to hurt her with actual knowledge of me.

And there it was, my moment of giving back.

Funny, I used to think I *was* a savior of sorts—or could be. If I've learned anything, though, it's that I'm just another asshole doing damage to the world. Beep figured that out long dark ages past, but, puzzle of puzzles, remained by my side.

I want to believe it's her real love I'm trying to celebrate in these woods, lovely, dark and deep. But the evidence suggests something darker; at best, an unhealthy codependence, at worst, a desire to be punished for crimes we've both imagined.

Enough of her. There's so very much to mourn, the rising whine lifts all remorse, leaving any single regret to drown. I've got a deal, a promise to keep, a few hundred yards to go before I sleep.

Rocking ick's cradle behind passing jeeps, the rough beast and I slouch toward Bethlehem. There are no force fields, no tripwires, no sensors to alert the armed forces, only hastily erected tents whose window-flaps radiate with inner lights and an open space with semi-circled tanks centered on all of the above.

Atop, where the ground goes flat for as far as the dark lets me see, I voodoo a déjà vu. The lay of the land, the shapes of the trees, are all just familiar enough for me to think, or at least pretend, that this was Joe's chicken farm; that those gray rot-wood buildings I spied in the viddy background once stood where I stand. That here, even pancakes can be real.

To put a final shine on it, way, way, up in the locked vault of the heavens, among the stars, I spy, with my little eye, something breaking the moon's roundness. What, though? A ship? A shadow? A mote in my eye? Whatever it is, ick trembles as if in love.

Ready or not, we've arrived.

# 13

The thing about actually being here? Now, I'm not all that sure it's where I want to be. I mean, shit, that's a fucking alien ship up there. Maybe I should take a year or two to think it over, let the adolescent haze get less dazed and confused before I do anything stupid. Anything *else* stupid, there already being a death and all.

My fellow traveler disagrees, vehemently. Abandoning the magic eight-ball bubbles, ick again takes to annexing my head. It's a heady rush, a furious blur, a storming of gates garlic-pressed into a thousand words that aren't quite a sentence, so harsh it devolves my own thinking; pancakes, monsters, dark woods, light hearts, stars and garters, explosions, friends and foes, full genres shelved in bookstore sections heretofore unimaginable, enlightenment masked as entertainment, entertainment using enlightenment as sparkly façade, and no way to tell one from the other.

Only the rumble of more tanks, sealing their circle beneath the moon, gives pause.

I go low, low, low. Knees to Mother Earth, hands parting brother bush, eyes peering at cousin military, I whisper so softly I barely hear myself:

"Slow down! I can't tell which part's you and which is my brain throwing up!"

Ick's instructions are simple, but also cold and impatient.

"Ask, then listen, idiot. If I'm bubbling, it means *I'm* speaking, if not, it's on you."

"Alright. What *do* you say, ick?"

The rush resumes, but a single thread is hog-tied to the pulsing in my arms:

"I say, go, go, go. I say we're almost there. I say you can't stop now. I say we had a deal."

"Hold it, gunkaroo. *I* say, Beep's dead. I say death wasn't part of the deal."

I'm cut off. "Not my fault! Yours. You're the idiot who flicked me her way."

"I've already lost track. Was that you, or me feeling guilty?"

A moment's quiet before: "Stupid, stupid, stupid! There are always at least three options. It was both of us. Of course, I feel like you, when I'm using your brain I can *only* feel like you. But you, you can't shut-up for more than two words. This is why we don't have nicer long-chat things!"

I muster my huffy. "You don't have to be rude about it, oh great, interstellar consciousness. I have gotten us this far."

"I do! I do have to be rude! Weren't you listening just now? You're all I have to work with, ergo, I have to be rude. If I had eyes, I'd glare until you got with the program."

"Ouchie and touché."

"Cut the 'tude! Stop playing absolute elsewhere! Go, go, go! We had a deal."

"Fine! Fine! But go where? I can't just carry you out into that field for a rendezvous with Rama, it's surrounded. How do we get to your ship?"

"Ship? What ship? OMG, you idiot. That's a moon dog, a parselene, an artifice, a… a…. Why can't you remember the damn word? It's only three syllables. A… a…"

"A distraction?"

"Yes, thanks. Go, go, go. Left, left, left. It's all alone and waiting. We had a deal."

I have eyes but cannot see. "*What's* to the left? Something to take you home?"

Ick has no mouth, yet ick must scream. "Fine! Fine! Yes! Close enough!"

"Is it… safe?"

"You're not in physical danger. You can't be. Never were."

A clearly me-thought giddies. "Why? Is it because I'm special? I *knew* it!"

"Fine! Fine! Yes. Close enough. Get me there. We had a deal.

I'll tell you all I know, at least all you could possibly understand. What the hell, you're not doing anything else, are you?"

Pity-puddle's got a point. Besides, much as I try to wheedle more info, all I get is a few stilted variations on, "Shut-up and do as you're told."

This is what it must've been like for Beep when she talked to me. A comeuppance for the way I treated her? No, but it explains why I tolerated her so long; the only other option was to be alone with myself.

Alrighty, then, left, left, left it is.

While, of course, I didn't expect an alien communion-spot to be anything I could expect, it is not what I expected. To strain the term once more, it's not even the *sort* of unexpected I expected. Nestled in a copse, concealed from the guarded, open plain, lies a flat concrete platform with a standing charcoal grill, just like any of the many from Blear, land of a thousand picnic tables.

"Go, go, go. Put me on it."

"The grill? You'll just drip all over everything."

"The flat part. The griddle."

Turns out there is no restaurant at the end of the universe. You have to cook for yourself. Never meet your heroes. Never realize your dreams. Never doubt the value of clichés.

I blink and frown so very much, I have to force myself to stop. "Seriously? What, are you like alien pancake mix or something, ick?"

"Seriously? What? No. Stop, just stop. We're so close, don't make me try to explain. Just take a few more damn steps and..."

"Shelley."

Beep's loss is far too fresh for me to be startled, but old enough for me to know her name-calling isn't real. I'm either hearing it from a dream, or she's joined the heavenly choir in my head. I assume, then, that thinking is enough to answer:

*Not, now, mon Beep.*

"Shelley?" she asks again.

The question makes no sense. *Of course, I'm Shelley, sweet phantasm. Now go away, I'll talk to you-in-myself later.*

"Shelley!"

A flustered ick clears me up: "For the love of... she's not in your head, idiot, she's standing behind you."

It's true! She's alive, bruised, bleeding in spots, but alive. Beep is alive! Alive and free, free to live out the rest of her dull existence before succumbing to Alzheimer's or some other ill of the flesh! Now, I don't have to feel guilty!

My emotions run so fast and deep, I don't think I can find the words, but I do. Undefended and unafraid at last, I say them right to her mop-top face.

"Hey, Beep. Not dead, huh?"

Admittedly, it loses in translation.

Before we are allowed a tearful, inappropriately groping hug, ick sticks his goo in.

"Of course, she is. Go, go, go!"

"Wait, you *knew* she was alive? Why didn't you tell me?"

"You didn't ask. You assumed. And when you assume, you make an ass..."

Everyone set on being rude today, Beep talks over the aphorism. "You could have checked for a body."

A bit abashed, I nod. "True, but in my defense, there was an awful lot of smoke and burning."

"I know. I was in it."

As if her story somehow requires proof beyond her word and charcoal smell, she coughs.

I offer a wide, magnanimous grin. "Oh, forget who abandoned who, silly, you're here now! I mean, sure, who knows how you got here, or what possessed you to follow, but..."

Her overall tone is not friendly. "I was forced."

"Oh."

I notice the jacket wrapped around her pants-lessness. It's Dick's. A parting gift? Nope. The scrupled drug lord emerges with a new gun all his own. In his other hand, he carries a bucket. It's not as large or nice as our tub, but neither is ick anymore.

Ick transmits the equivalent of, "Ah, shit. This is exactly what I wanted to avoid."

"Dick, look at you! Look at both of you, here, in the middle of the woods, surrounded by tanks! Don't get me wrong, it fits, in a crappy cliché-ridden kind of way, despite the whole *how the fuck did you get here* plot-hole."

Beep minds the gap. "Handy-girl plopped a tracer in ick back in Blear."

I look down at ick. "And you felt this wasn't worth mentioning, either?"

If glop could shrug, it would. "I thought it was some kind of human toy."

I have choice words for ick, but it's Dick turn to be rude.

"Who the fuck is Handy-girl? You know what? Never mind." He kicks the bucket our way. "Sudsy-wudsy goes in there now."

Before I can complement him on the clever name choice, Dick pulls back the thingy on the gun, you know, the part that spring-slams the casing to ignite the gunpowder and send the slug spinning down the barrel. The hammer, I believe it's called.

Twisting the gun sideways, he seems to be using the Center Lock Axis. Created by Kent Police Officer Paul Castle, and since popularized by John Wick and gangstas alike, it's not simply a stance, it's an intricate shooting system designed to improve hit rate.

I doubt Dick knows that, 'cause he pushes the barrel into Beep's temple so hard, it's like he's trying to avoid using bullets at all, by forcing it through the bone. Probably just thinks holding the gun sideways looks cool. It's certainly cool enough for the prodigal Beep.

She winces mightily.

"Ever see someone shot in the head? I have. Films and TV, they don't get it quite right."

Poor thing's had a long day. She's got the shakey-shakes, but still manages to speak.

"Shelley, just... let him shoot me. I don't want to live like this anymore."

That can't be right. She can't mean that. It'd be like going to a party without being invited. Is it a ruse, intended to distract Dick? Does she expect me to leap upon him the instant he expresses surprise, and in a frantic rush of mad teen adrenaline, wrest the dread weapon away and win the day?

It doesn't seem like a ruse. Besides, lizard-king Dick doesn't so much as blink. Sad to say, I've no tricks left, no last-minute cards to play. Only one alien and one Beep to go around.

Fuck. It's a choice.

You'd think that having just lived in a Beep-less world, it'd be a quick, easy choice, but that experience only makes it harder. I mean, I thought her gone, but thar she blows. How do I know it won't happen that way again?

Oh, fine. I take too long, but I get there. Hating myself all the way, I lower ick into the bucket. It's over. I don't feel defeated. More like there was never a fight. If I have a shred of insight about this, it dies on the thief-laden route between my brain and my mouth.

Ick doesn't bubble and boil, so much as wriggle. I'd no idea he had moves that were, well, not like Jagger, more like frustrated worms.

"We had a deal!"

"I know, ick, I know. No one's more surprised at this turn of events than I."

I'm wrong about that. Beep's pretty shocked, too, which I kinda understand, given the depth of my sacrifice. The big shocker is that tonight's winner of the Wide-Eyed with Surprise award goes to Dick. He regards the procedure as nothing short of miraculous.

"It *listens* to you?"

"I use she/her pronouns, Dick."

As he, full of wonder, approaches the bucket, I circle around him. For a moment, we're close enough for me to breathe my final words against his cheek.

"We'll have our Reichenbach Falls yet, James."

Slapping them off as if a bug, he grabs the bucket and lifts, ready to go.

I sidle up to Beep, two peas without an escape pod.

She's stunned in a way that's downright offensive. "Shelley, why did you...?"

"Short answer? Because I've no desire to be responsible for your fate."

"*You?* Responsible for *me?*"

But endings have a way of not ending at all.

The bucket trembles in Dick's sweaty hands. He doesn't notice at first, while I assume it's the usual bubbles that indicate ick's irritation, or, worse, that they express the fear of any animal en route to the slaughterhouse. More than a rolling shudder, it becomes a downright shaking, a rattling that makes it hard for Dick to hold onto the bucket at all.

I think I hear ick saying, "We had a deal!"

But no, this time it's me, trying to make sense of the bucking pail.

"We had a deal!"

That was ick. About to cry? To whimper and further break my already shattered heart? No. I sense no sadness, no terror, just the betrayed anger implicit in, "We had a deal!"

And then, well....

...ick eats Dick.

# 14

Yep. That about sums it up. Ick eats Dick.

One second, ick's in the bucket, the next, ick's all over Dick, tearing away with those tiny fishbone parts, which now I'm guessing are... teeth?

It's fast, and not much to look at. I mean, you know me, I'm all about capturing the sublime majesty of the moment. This? Meh. Dick doesn't even have time to scream. He gets out a little sound, but it's more like the opening squeak of a laid-back "Huh? What's up with this?" than anything shriek-like. There's some blood, but the goo cleans it up as it goes along. Trust me, you're not missing much.

Beep, far more compassionate than I, says only, "Okay, then."

(In her case, though, she may be going into shock.)

I guess this means Dick wasn't my nemesis. Oh, well. Can't be right all the time. So, what was he in this cosmic omelet? If we are to be judged by our end, nothing more than a meal. I hope it was a happy one. Interestingly, the glop seems no larger, making me wonder where ick puts it all.

All copacetic, loose-ends tied, I step forward to reclaim ick and, at long last, throw the one true ring into Mount Doom, take ET home, or whatever.

The SOBlob hisses. Fishbones poke my way.

Given Dick's quick departure, I step back. "Whoa! Ick, buddy! What's up with that?"

The answer's loud and clear. "You broke our deal."

"Oh, come on! He was going to kill Beep! It was a morality test, and I passed. You can't punish me for passing a morality test!"

Ick, much more mobile than it let on, makes for the post holding the grill. It's like watching a giant snail move, but without the shell, or the snail, just the slime-trail.

Furious, I kick some dirt on it. "You're going to ditch me on a technicality? I got you this far, snot-face! Let's finish it! Fair's fair, and don't give me any shit about fairness being a human concept."

Ick goes smug. "Concept is a human concept."

No longer loving the alien, I make a face. "Oh, very inciteful, smarty-ick. You knew enough about fairness to make the deal in the first place, didn't you? I've suffered for this! I've made Beep suffer for it! 90% of the job deserves 90% of the pay, no?"

"No!"

"Agh!" I want to pull my hair out, or maybe Beep's. Someone's hair has got to go. "How about a little something for my troubles? An alien half-truth? An ill-phrased aphorism?"

"No!"

Rebuffed, I turn to Beep. "This is *your* fault for getting caught with your pants down!"

"Well, no, that was you."

"You're taking *its* side? After it almost got you killed?"

"That was you, too. But, maybe, for once, just let it go? Let *ick* go?"

"Look deep into my eyes, old chum, stare long and hard. Anything in there, anything at all, make you think I'm going to let this go? That live and let live is a capability I've kept hidden all these years?"

"No," she submits.

Ick reaches the base. Two feet up and he'll be free of our ridiculous species.

"Ick, please! Don't leave me like this, don't leave me here with Beep! It's not good for either of us!"

As I plead, the heartless goo circles the post, pools and oozes upward a bit. Fishbones curl and try to gain purchase. So many, so sticky, it should be easy-peasy, but, with the quietest of clicking... they fail. The process repeats, with more fishbones, but the results are the same.

Ick can't do it, it can't. I don't laugh so much as cackle hysterically.

"Well, well, well." Hands on thighs, I lower myself for a closer look. "Need a hand to hop on the barbie?"

"Yes… please…."

I go into a slow clap and cackle some more. "There's your hand, ick. Get it? Have you grasped the complexity of human humor or do I have to explain it?"

"Shitty joke. You suck. Fine, fine, fine. We have a deal. Again."

"Alrighty, then!" I slither my arms beneath one last time.

"Shelley, wait."

"Fucking Beep, god damn it! WHAT?"

"I just want you to know, I'm sorry."

My brow furrows like a relief map of the Martian Canals. "By the great Cthulhu, as you pointed out a few seconds ago. I'm the one who left you to die, remember?"

She backs away, face growing pale until it seems to fade in the dark.

"Right. Sure. Go ahead."

Tut-tutting my disapproval, I place ick. The only surprise is that there are no further interruptions. The griddle-plate not quite level, the drooping goop gathers along one side, then stills.

"You good, ick?"

"Yes. Ready?"

I straighten and enter the moment, a moment in which I know everything's about to change forever, but I've no idea how. It's not unlike the instant before I first saw ick. As mentioned, it is here, in this oh-so-special in-between, zero-g-spot, that the mind, free of expectation, is closest to reality. The wise would probably try to linger, dwell in uncertainty as long as possible. Not me. I only want to hear whatever the fuck it is ick has to tell me.

"Ready. Lay it on me, big guy."

"Well," ick says, "for starters, you're dead."

Wait. What? I repeat it out loud. "Wait. What?"

"You're dead."

That's a puzzler. "You mean like all humanity is spiritually dead?"

"No. Not spiritually."

"I'm not following. Do you mean like, the rest of humanity is gone, and as the sole survivor I'm embracing a fantasy that everyone is still is alive to keep myself from going mad?"

"Closer," Ick says. "But it's the other way around."

Purely as an exercise in abstraction, I turn the concept on its head.

"*I'm* dead, but embracing a fantasy that I'm alive?"

"That's the one. Bingo."

"I'm *dead*? *I'm* dead? Like a ghost?"

"Yep, yep and yep. As far as you can understand, anyway. Deal's done. I'll be going now."

"Wait! No! There's nothing dead or ghostly about me. People see me! We talk and everything."

"Haven't you noticed how everyone ignores you?"

"Sure, some, but I simply assumed they weren't very discerning."

"Or how you can't touch anything?"

"Why on earth would I want to touch anything when I have Beep? And I do *so* touch stuff. I carried you!"

"That's because I'm not entirely physical, and you're not physical *at all*. Which is why you don't get all wonky. It's why I agreed to this stupid deal in the first place. Can I go now?"

"What about Beep? She talks to me."

"She's special."

"*Beep's* special? Seriously?"

"Well, to you, anyway."

"How? How is *she* special? Like she's my bestie, so the grave itself couldn't sever our friendship?"

"Uh… I'll let her handle that one. I'm gonna…"

"Can you tell me how it happened? How I died?"

"Mmm. Not really my place."

A brow-frowning Beep opens her mouth. Words come out. "How could you not know?"

"What, that you're special?" I harrumph. "I hardly think this the time for self-aggrandizement!"

"No, how you died."

"You know? You've known? You knew? *How*? Was I drinking and driving? Was I texting and driving? Was I texting, drinking and driving? Was I at least behind a wheel? No, of course not, I only have a learner's permit and I'd never risk..."

"That was ten years ago. I'm twenty-six, and, oh god, still living with my parents."

"So... no driver's test next month?"

Fishbones tap like fingertips, producing a series of tsk-tsks aimed my way. "You think you understand so much, but you don't know a thing about your own, what's the word? Friend."

I turn on her. Oh, how I turn. "Beep? *You* killed me because you were driving and texting? Is that why you've felt guilty all this time?"

Her voice goes funny in a not-ha-ha-ha way. "It wasn't an accident."

"You lost control of the wheel?"

"There were no cars involved!" Lips aquiver, her throat erupts. "It was only you and me."

I feel as if she's trying to tell me something. "Are you saying... you killed me on purpose? Why, Beep, *why*? Was it shame over your lesbian lust for me, because you know, given my bod, no court of god or man would..."

"No! No! No! I've told you a billion times, I'm bi, but I've never, ever been into you."

"Then what possible reason..."

Eyes, wide and bloodshot, stream tears. "Aside from the fact you were always so mean to me? Aside from the fact that everything was always, completely totally about you? You want to know what finally did it? I'll tell you. You *never ever* shut up! I was so sick of your yammering, I'd do anything, *anything*, to end it!"

"Yammering? That's harsh."

She goes into a creepy, choking laugh. "And the real joke? I actually thought killing you would do it, that I'd finally, finally get some quiet. But, no. You're still fucking here, aren't you? And you're still fucking talking! For pity's sake, a shit-ass *alien* can't stop you."

Sobbing wet and wild, she sinks to uncovered knees. "It's my punishment, I know I deserve it, but dear God, why can't you ever just shut the fuck-up?"

The straws I grasp are imaginary, but I grasp them nonetheless. "So... did I like, fall down the steps and you didn't call for help?"

"No! I covered your head with a pillow and held it there until your arms turned blue. It took like, an hour. It was the last time I ever felt... happy."

"I see. How sad for you. Why didn't you ever tell me?"

"I tried, for like a year, but you wouldn't listen. After that, I gave up. I don't know how ghosts work. I figured if you weren't supposed to know, rubbing your nose in it would be like killing you all over again, and it's not like that worked out well for me the first time, is it?"

I've no counter argument, no leg to stand on, literally, since, apparently, I have no legs.

"You've got your great secret," ick says. "Satisfied?"

"No," I say.

"Good."

"But what do I do now, oh, ick, what do I do?"

"How do I know? Go be a ghost-girl detective for all I care. I'm done here."

The tone, clear as a bell, is full of a contempt and loathing that is not at all my own.

Ick's vanishing is as quick and dull as the eating of Dick. A *pht* and nothing more.

Well played, ick, well played.

I look past the tip of my nose, into a dark that embraces both the alien and the familiar equally. There, I catch a fleeting glimpse of more than just myself, an honest hint of others, an eternal, everlasting legion of them. I try to hold the moment, the emptiness warm to my touch. While it lasts, as long as it lasts, I wonder why the dark among them are so easy to see, the light so obscure.

Then I'm back where we started, alone with Beep again.

Drained, she rises, sniffs and wipes her face with Dick's jacket sleeve.

I try to smile. "I guess this means... I'm *your* imaginary friend?"

A nod, of sorts, a sort of nod.

Funny how you can pray for change, and when it finally comes, it doesn't really change anything at all. At least I didn't lie at the beginning. It was a ghost story all along.

# 15

We hunt the ghosts,
       We hunt ourselves.

It's not so bad. My asthma's gone. And people cannot misjudge what they cannot see.

Maybe I *should* become a detective.

Ghost Girl and Beep, the Further Adventures of.

What do you think?

# About the Author

Born in the Bronx, Stefan Petrucha spent his formative years moving between the big city and the suburbs, both of which made him prefer escapism. A fan of comic books, science fiction and horror since learning to read, in high school and college he added a love for all sorts of literary work, eventually learning that the very best fiction always brings you back to reality, so, really, there's no way out.

Curious about other Crossroad Press books?
Stop by our site:
http://store.crossroadpress.com
We offer quality writing
in digital, audio, and print formats.

Enter the code FIRSTBOOK
to get 20% off your first order from our store!
Stop by today!

www.ingramcontent.com/pod-product-compliance
Lightning Source LLC
Chambersburg PA
CBHW061252170626
46809CB00007B/2955